How to Bake a Cupcake

How to Bake a Cupcake

H.L. Sweatte

Jasmine Girl Publishing

www.JGirlPub.com

Johnnie Girl Publishing

Johnnie Girl Books are published by
Johnnie Girl Publishing
39270 Paseo Padre Parkway #415
Fremont, CA 94538
www.JGirlPub.com

How to Bake a Cupcake is a work of fiction. The characters, organizations, locales and incidents portrayed in this tale are either products of the author's imagination, or are used fictitiously. Any resemblance to actual persons living or dead is purely coincidental.

ISBN: 978-0-6152-3993-4
LCCN: 2008934208

Printed in the United States of America

This book is dedicated to my family and friends, who have supported me throughout the years. I must also give special thanks to my husband for believing in me and providing me the opportunity to spread my wings…

Always in loving memory of Johnnie Mae Rivers.

CHAPTER 1

"Jackson and Jasmine Taylor, I like the sound of that." He took a long sip of his coffee and stared at her intensely with those deep, dark eyes of his. She held his gaze for a moment, but then his eyes started to wander, as he examined every inch of her being.

Jackson was a lion, more ferocious than the others. Jasmine didn't like being pursued, especially like this—so steadily and aggressively. In the past she would have simply felt flattered, but had made it a point to steer clear of Jackson Taylor, the man rumored to be a womanizer. Yet, he hadn't allowed her unflattering reputation to deter him from trying to claim her as his prize. In fact, he seemed to be turned on by it. If she hadn't already scoped out the dean's son, Stacey Fisher, as her target, perhaps she would have given Jackson a chance—a real chance that is.

"Excuse me," Jasmine replied in a forceful tone before sliding past Jackson to give the barista her order.

"I'll take a tall espresso!" Practically shouting at the girl behind the counter, Jasmine attempted to make her voice heard over all the chatter taking place around them. Café Milano, located right across the street from the south side of UC Berkeley's campus, was always busy, and this day was no exception. After all, finals were looming, so everyone was getting their caffeine fix to keep them up through what would undoubtedly be a long study night. As she stood at the counter waiting for her order, Jasmine could feel Jackson's eyes pierce the back of her skull.

"That's a pretty strong drink for someone so petite." Ignoring his comment, Jasmine continued to wait patiently for her order. Not one to be ignored, Jackson moved in closer behind her. He stood so close that she could smell his cologne—Issey Miyake, the same brand Demetri used to wear. At $72.00 a pop, that was an expensive scent for a college student. Jasmine knew because she used to buy 4.2-ounce bottles for Demetri regularly, while most teens her age could barely afford one. Yet, it was clear to her and anyone who had eyes to see that Jackson wasn't an ordinary college boy. A graduate student at the Haas School of Business, working on obtaining his MBA, Jackson wasn't a boy at all— Jackson was a man.

After giving the barista exact change for her coffee, Jasmine gathered her belongings and began to head toward the door, but of course, Jackson had to stand in front of her with his legs spread shoulder-width apart, and block her path. She was forced to face those deep, dark eyes yet again, as he stared at her and took a bite out of a delectably large cupcake that seemed to appear out of nowhere. "Will you be my study partner for the night?" he asked, grinning devilishly before raising his cup to take another sip of coffee.

What a cocky bastard. Jasmine tried to come up with a witty response to his flirtatious question, but caught a glimpse of Stacey entering the café out of the corner of her eye, and suddenly, all thoughts shifted towards him. Her heart revved up like she had just finished a ten-yard dash. Taking a deep breath, she looked past Jackson in order to follow her soon-to-be honey's every move.

"Excuse me," said Jasmine, completely abandoning the thought of engaging him in a game of ping-pong wit.

Aware that her attention had averted from him, Jackson took a step back, then looked over his shoulder to follow the path Jasmine's eyes had taken. He saw Stacey and smirked. "I'm surprised you didn't order a *small* coffee with lots of sugar and cream," he said mockingly, referring to her light-skinned, curly-haired, object of affection.

"Don't hate," she replied, as she pushed past him and began walking toward Stacey.

Jasmine hurriedly attempted to maneuver her way through the sea of tables and chairs that occupied the café. She wanted to make it over to Stacey before anyone else clamored around him. Yet, before she could make it just two feet away from Jackson, David Sims, one of the star athletes on Cal's football team, jumped in front of her and asked if she needed help carrying her things. His wide body blocked her view of Stacey, and she immediately became annoyed.

"No thank you," Jasmine replied, irritated, yet still trying to sound polite. If it were any other day, she would have stopped to flirt with David, as she did with most of the guys who showered her with attention. This time however, Stacey was the only boy on her mind, and she so desperately wanted to talk to him.

Without even looking David in the eye, Jasmine slinked past him and continued to head toward Stacey. Unfortunately, some beady-eyed girl beat her to him, and she watched as the unidentified young lady smiled and giggled at everything Stacey said, while flaunting what appeared to be newly-whitened teeth. Unfortunately for her, Jasmine already had her game plan mapped out, and it involved a lot more than a recent trip to the dentist.

"Stacey," Jasmine chimed, while sliding in between him and his female companion. "I didn't think I'd see you here. After all, your score on Professor Murphy's last quiz proves you're more than ready for the final." Feeling absolutely no shame for having interrupted what she had deemed to be a meaningless conversation, Jasmine remained unaffected by the stunned look on the girl's face as she continued to talk to Stacey.

"Hey Jazz," Stacey replied with a huge grin. Seeing those dimples she adored practically forced Jasmine to fall into a trance. "I'm not here to study," he continued, "I actually just stopped by to drop off some lecture notes to a friend." Stacey pointed toward the young lady who stood behind Jasmine with mouth agape. Unknowingly adding to his friend's frustration, he asked Jasmine how she was doing, then pulled her into a hug. Jasmine, aware of her power to intimidate, purposely squeezed Stacey tightly before cocking her head to the side to shoot a look at his friend. It didn't take long for her to get the point, because she quickly scurried away.

"Wait!" Stacey called out to his buddy as he slowly released Jasmine from his embrace, but she was already on her way out the door.

"Don't mind her," said Jasmine, dismissively waving her hand in the air. "So, I was wondering, do you have time to go over a few probability questions with me for the stat final?"

"Sorry Jazz," Stacey replied before glancing down at his watch. "I have a meeting with the coach in a few. Besides, you're a smart girl, I'm sure you can figure them out. In fact, you could probably teach me a thing or two."

Stacey was right; Jasmine was a smart girl, but she'd be willing to play dumb if it meant she could spend more time with him.

Before she could think of something to say that would persuade him to reconsider, Stacy placed one hand on her shoulder and said, "I gotta bounce, Jazz, but it was good seeing you, as always."

"You too," she replied, feeling a little disappointed.

Stacey took a few steps toward the door, then turned around and added, "Say hello to Missy for me, will you?"

"I will," Jasmine assured, smiling faintly. It pained her to watch him leave so soon, which is why she convinced herself that his hectic schedule and nothing else, was the reason for his early departure. After all, Stacey was a busy guy. Between classes, football, and working alongside his father in the dean's office, did he really have much time to devote to a social life? Whether he truly did or not, one thing was certain: Stacey was extremely popular with the ladies and the men. The ladies adored him because he was fine, intelligent, and extremely ambitious. Guys liked him because he was cool, athletic, and basically everything they aspired to be.

As Jasmine watched Stacey exit via the double doors of the café, she couldn't help but feel a little defeated. Yet, tomorrow was another day, and she had a lot more tricks up her sleeve.

CHAPTER 2

Asking Stacey for help with her studies was really a desperate move on Jasmine's part, because he knew, as did everyone else, that she was an A student. She wasn't even stressed out about finals like most of her peers, and was extremely confident in her ability to handle whatever her professors had to dish out. That's why instead of killing herself trying to cram like most of the students at Cal, Jasmine decided to put in extra hours at Pleasant Beginnings, the assisted living facility where she volunteered. Yet, had she known putting in more hours at the facility meant receiving more lectures from Missy Mae Holden, the Pleasant Beginnings resident she catered to, Jasmine would have opted to stay in her apartment and review some of the probability questions she spoke to Stacey about.

"So, how are you getting along in school?" asked Missy before grabbing the remote control from the nightstand next to her bed. Her favorite soap opera had just ended, so she was now ready to turn off the television and give Jasmine her undivided attention.

"My classes are cool and grades are good. Final exams are next week, so everyone is busy studying right now."

"Well, shouldn't you be off studying too?"

"Nah. I've done all the studying I'm gonna do."

"You sound confident, as always. You know I'm always bragging about you to my friends. Beauty and brains; two things I like to see in a young woman. You're like the daughter I never had."

"Aw, thanks Missy," Jasmine replied, knowing that Missy really meant it.

"But…"

I should have known there'd be a "but."

"I just wish you'd stop chasing after these boys the way that you do. You know they don't like aggressive girls. Back in my day, a young lady would sit back and allow a man to be a man. You know, chase her. Shoot, I wish I would catch you chasing after these boys, I'd spank you good."

"Here you go," said Jasmine, while setting Missy's lunch tray down in front of her.

"Don't try to distract me with this food! You know you hear me."

"Yes, ma'am, I hear you. But, I'll have you know that I'm not chasing after *these boys*. There's only one boy I like, and his name is—"

"Stacey Fisher, I know," interrupted Missy, rolling her eyes. "So, you're not chasing *boys*, you're chasing *a boy*. When are you going to realize that that boy don't want you? If he did, he would have asked you out by now. But no, you have to keep prancing yourself around in front of him, as if he don't already see you."

Missy always told it like it was, something that many people may have found off-putting. Yet Jasmine, who at times had also found Missy's blunt remarks to be annoying, chose to ignore their sting because she knew better than anyone that they came from a loving place. Besides, she wasn't going to argue with someone in Missy's condition.

Missy was still trying to recover from a stroke she'd suffered a few months back. Although she had regained her speech, her mobility was still very limited. Thus, she stayed in bed most of the time, but was visited by a physical therapist who had been desperately trying to help her walk again. As far as Jasmine was concerned, it all seemed futile in a sense, because Missy appeared to be pretty content lying in bed all day while watching her "stories" and having everyone on staff, including Jasmine, cater to her.

Keeping Missy happy was definitely part of Jasmine's job, which she accomplished for the most part. She mainly kept her spirits up and tried not to upset her, which went back to why she didn't want to argue with her. However, she did feel somewhat compelled to attempt a better explanation for her interaction with Stacey.

"I actually bumped into Stacey yesterday at a café," said Jasmine, averting her eyes from Missy's. "He was all smiles when he saw me. We have one class together this semester, but I don't get to talk to him much during lecture. I think that's why he was so happy to see me. He even gave me a hug. Oh, and he told me to tell you, 'Hi.'"

Jasmine looked down at her hands as she began to smooth imaginary wrinkles out of the uniform all volunteers at Pleasant Beginnings were required to wear. Knowing that she was really trying to avoid eye contact with her, Missy didn't respond. Instead, the silence forced Jasmine to look at her and sure enough, she found Missy peering at her over the rim of her glasses while taking a sip of the apple juice she had served her. Her expression was proof that she didn't buy it.

"So, he asked you out, huh?"

"Um, not really," Jasmine replied. She felt her cheeks grow warm, then quickly added, "He was in a hurry…he had to see his football coach. He'll probably ask me out when I see him again."

"And when will that be?"

"Next weekend. One of the fraternities is throwing a big end-of-semester party. Everyone's gonna be there."

"Yeah well, you just make sure that you let him approach you. Don't go running up to him and make a fool of yourself like you did last year."

Missy was referring to freshman orientation, where Jasmine first laid eyes on Stacey. When she had asked Jasmine how the two of them met, Jasmine explained how she walked over and introduced herself to him once the panel discussion with upperclassmen ended. Missy considered Jasmine's actions bold and desperate, whereas she simply saw them as taking initiative.

"You remind me of this girl they got on *The Young and the Restless*. She's always scheming to get some man or take someone else's."

Jasmine usually found it funny whenever Missy would compare someone she knew to a soap opera character, but when she did it to her, it didn't seem so funny. "I'm not *scheming* to do anything," she assured Missy, who was almost finished with her meal. "As far as I know, Stacey's not seeing anyone."

"I hope not, for your sake," stated Missy, frowning. "For once I wish you would allow yourself to fall for someone who is sincere, someone who is available both physically and emotionally. You've met some nice young men since you've been here, but for some reason are so stuck on Stacey that you can't see straight." She paused to adjust her glasses before continuing. "Just because Demetri hurt you—"

"Demetri has nothing to do with this!" Jasmine snapped, cutting Missy short. Missy's head jerked back like she'd just been slapped, so Jasmine modified her tone before continuing. "Like I said, Stacey's a busy guy. I know he would be with me if he had time."

"Right," Missy replied in her usual, skeptical tone. "And until then, I'm sure you're going to make it a point to show him what he's missing."

You've got that right.

Missy and Jasmine may not have seen eye to eye on things, but that didn't stop Jasmine from wanting to be around her. Aside from upholding the values her father instilled in her about the importance of giving back to others—be it monetarily or in the form of community service, Jasmine succeeded in establishing a solid bond with Missy. A bond that surpassed the twenty hours of weekly care required of her volunteer duties.

Missy served as a mother figure, and quite often the voice of reason for Jasmine, who, like most young women her age, didn't have a firm grasp on life or her role in it. She was appreciative of Missy's guidance, and relied on it more than Missy would ever know. It was therefore easy for Jasmine to devote time and energy toward caring for her, because she didn't expect anything in return outside of the love, respect, and admiration that was already bestowed upon her freely. Missy was rare in that sense, for she simply valued companionship, and didn't seek to gain anything such as money or social perks like so many others who had come and gone in Jasmine's life. It was her genuine nature that enabled Jasmine to let down her guard and be vulnerable in ways that she would never be with anyone else.

Knowing how much Missy enjoyed her company, Jasmine decided to spend an extra two hours with her that day, as they continued to talk about the weather, other residents at the facility, and just life in general. Then, before the sun set, they said their goodbyes, and Jasmine headed home.

Chapter 3

Finals went well as Jasmine expected, so her father and Missy had one more thing to be proud about. It was now time for her to treat herself, and the fact that one of the biggest parties of the year was about to take place provided more incentive for her to splurge. It was a Saturday afternoon and she was at the mall scouting out the perfect dress to wear that evening. It had to be something that displayed her assets without looking trashy. It had to be an attention grabber, something that announced her presence. Most importantly, it had to be something that Stacey would like.

After browsing inside of Caché, Nordstrom, and Express with no luck, Jasmine's eyes finally zoned in on the perfect number as she approached Bebe: a red, low-cut, knee-length wrap dress. *Perfect!* Shortly after entering the store, Jasmine walked out with a new dress in hand. Like most of the high-end stores in her hometown of Los Angeles, the sales people at Bebe knew her by name, so the transaction was swift. This was mainly due to the fact that she had what most young college girls didn't: daddy's credit card with no limit. Missy always said that if she had a mother in her life to teach her discipline, she wouldn't be so lucky. Yet, Missy failed to realize that Jasmine's current spending habits actually paled in comparison to her expenditures of the past.

No longer was Jasmine shopping for fake girlfriends who used her to boost their social clout as she helped give new life to their otherwise pallid wardrobes. Similarly, she was no longer shopping for the men in her life because unlike Demetri, who proved to be her longest relationship to date, they came and went like yesterday's news and therefore didn't merit any gift giving. That selfless lifestyle laden with naïveté had gotten her nowhere in the past, and she was a changed woman because of it. Deep down she was still the same old Jasmine, but on the surface she was a lot tougher, harder, and wiser…or so she thought.

"Hello daddy…" Jasmine's voice trailed off as she sang a warm greeting to her father after dialing his number on the diamond-encrusted cell phone she kept clipped to her hip. "I just want to let you know that I had to pick something up at the mall. There's a party tonight, and I didn't have anything to wear."

"That's fine honey," her father replied. "Although, I highly doubt there was nothing in your closet for you to wear."

"Well, you know how it is," Jasmine joked with a grin. She was voted best dressed all four years of high school, so wardrobe problems had never been an issue for her. Her father knew that, and therefore found his daughter's remark humorous.

"Yeah, I '*know how it is*,'" he replied, chuckling. Mr. Fairchild had no problem with Jasmine's frequent trips to the mall, especially since she had decided to no longer support her "friends" on his credit. In fact, he was proud to attribute his lower monthly credit card balance to her "newfound sense of self." Besides, for a man of his wealth, money was no object, for all that mattered to him was his daughter's well being. She was now four hundred miles away from home—a distance he found heartwrenching. Yet, he tried hard to stay strong for his "little princess," the only lady in his life since his wife's passing. "So, when are you coming home?" he asked, trying to quell the angst in his voice.

"Well, that's what I was going to talk to you about. I was actually thinking about staying up here for the summer, maybe take some classes..."

"Why would you want to do that? You're not behind, are you?"

"No. I just thought it'd be a good idea."

"Hmm. Why do I get the feeling that there's something you're not telling me?" Her father paused for a moment, then said, "Or perhaps *someone* you're not telling me about?"

"Daddy, I know you're not accusing me of not having a mind of my own. Do you really think that someone could talk me into doing anything, let alone staying on campus for the summer?" Knowing that her words contradicted the moments in her past when she had allowed herself to be victimized by the powers of persuasion, Jasmine hoped her father wouldn't comment on her faux pas. The last thing she needed was a little salt in her wounds.

"Well, I guess not," he replied. "I almost forgot that Fisher's son is going to be busy training for next season, so he can't be the reason after all."

Football training? Mr. Fairchild definitely knew more about Stacey's schedule than his daughter because he and Mr. Fisher were associates. Jasmine's father made a living trading corporate bonds and had made so many charitable donations to Cal that he was practically its main sponsor. Jasmine was hoping to stick around for the summer to put in more time with Stacey and assumed he would be staying on campus to continue working in the dean's office, and therefore hadn't given his football training a single thought.

"Well daddy, I'll think about it some more and get back to you," Jasmine finally replied, trying to sound unfazed by the revelation.

"All right honey. Have fun tonight."

"I will daddy." *I'd better.*

Chapter 4

After ending her conversation with her father, Jasmine scurried over to the sidewalk to catch a cab ride home. She didn't own a car because parking was scarce in Berkeley and everything was centralized, so she could therefore easily walk to and from the grocery stores, the bank, the post office, and pretty much everywhere she needed to go. Back home in Los Angeles, it was almost impossible for her to get around without a car, which is why she was fortunate to have access to daddy's Jag, Rolls Royce, and shiny black Hummer whenever she was in town.

To get to places in the Bay Area that weren't within walking distance, Jasmine relied on cab services because buses and BART were out of the question as far as she was concerned. When riding public transportation, one never knows who one will have to sit next to. Cab rides therefore enabled Jasmine to ride in peace without having to be around crying babies, crazy drunks, and whatever other wacky types of people could be found sitting too close for comfort on the bus. She just had to hope and pray that the cab drivers weren't crazy because they didn't call the town "Berserk-ley," for nothing.

As soon as she made it back to her quaint, one-bedroom apartment located just a few blocks away from campus, Jasmine jumped in the shower to start primping for the party. She tried living in the dorms her freshman year, but after taking one look at the cramped space she would have been forced to share with some strange girl from Wisconsin, she made one phone call to daddy, and that was the end of that. Besides, she no longer trusted anybody and figured it was best that she live on her own.

Foxy, Jasmine's cat, was lying on the bed when she stepped out of the shower. Mr. Fisk, the apartment manager, didn't allow pets, but once Jasmine had explained to him that Foxy was well trained and had been de-clawed, he caved in. She had actually lied about Foxy being de-clawed, but could tell by the way Mr. Fisk was looking at her that day that she could have told him anything, and he would have believed it. Besides, who would de-claw a cat anyway? A cat's just not a cat without them.

"Come here sweetie pie," said Jasmine to Foxy while gathering her up in her arms. Foxy purred loudly as Jasmine stroked her tummy. "Yeah, I know what you like," she said before placing Foxy back on the bed so that she could finish getting ready.

After slipping into her new dress, Jasmine fished inside her purse for a pack of cigarettes. She didn't consider herself a smoker because she didn't smoke often. It was just a little habit she picked up during her junior year of high school. Some friends of hers thought smoking would make them seem cooler than they already were, so she started smoking after school and on the weekends. She never did it around her father, for he would have been furious to know she had been endangering her health in such a manner. Jasmine actually didn't like smoking at first, until she started noticing that it did help take the edge off. Considering that she was nervous and anxious about what was about to go down that evening, she needed a hit of a cig to keep her sane.

Foxy leaped off the bed and ran underneath it to hide as soon as she caught a whiff of smoke. She hated the smell, and Stacey did too, which is why Jasmine proceeded to douse herself with some of her most expensive perfume, and popped a few Altoids in an effort to hide any remnants of her nasty habit. It had only taken a few drags for her to feel calm, so she quickly smashed out the butt and headed over to the closet to scout out the perfect pair of shoes.

After putting on a pair of silver stilettos that strapped around the ankles, Jasmine stood in front of a full length mirror to examine her look. *It truly is perfect.* "If Stacey doesn't notice me in this dress, then he must be gay," she said to Foxy, who began weaving herself around her legs. She took her excitement as approval.

After grabbing her silver clutch purse, Jasmine kissed Foxy goodbye before heading outside to wait for the taxi she reserved. It didn't take long for the driver to arrive, and she anxiously hopped in and asked to be taken to the City Center Marriott in downtown Oakland. The party was being hosted by the PKG's, one of the more popular African American fraternities on campus. Jasmine was excited because they never failed to throw a great event.

The driver immediately started flirting with Jasmine once she entered the cab, but she did her best to keep the conversation at a minimum to stave off his advances. Having absolutely no interest in him or anything he had to say, her mind remained focused on one person only, and that was Stacey.

Before long, the driver pulled up in front of the hotel and Jasmine reached inside her purse to pull out a fifty dollar bill. After slipping it in between the driver's fingers, she told him to "Keep the change," then proceeded toward the hotel's main entrance where she was immediately greeted by balloons and signs that pointed toward the ballroom where the party was taking place. To her dismay, a long line had already formed, as people eagerly awaited access to the party. Having no intention of standing in the back of the line, Jasmine immediately began working her charm the moment she spotted Chris Baker, last year's summer fling. "Hey Chris, long time no see."

"Hi Jazz!" replied Chris enthusiastically. Chris had about fifty teeth, all of which could be seen whenever he smiled. "Why haven't you called me?"

"I've been busy with school and volunteering." *That was a lie.* "But, that doesn't mean that I've forgotten about you." *That was a lie too.* Chris and Jasmine had fun hanging out the previous summer, but their romance—if you can call it that, was very short lived. When Chris started talking about love and marriage, Jasmine knew it was time to kiss their relationship goodbye. She didn't trust her heart with anyone, especially those who came on too strong or tried to force the issue of commitment. She preferred to be in the driver's seat from now on, for she felt that it gave her some sort of power—an inability to be deceived.

"Well, my number hasn't changed, so feel free to use it," said Chris, who unfortunately thought Jasmine had suddenly regained a genuine interest in him.

"I will," she replied with the same smile that had a tendency to make boys' knees turn weak. Before she could weasel her way in front of Chris in line, Jasmine heard someone else call out her name.

"Hey Jasmine, over here! It's your boy, Eric!"

Whipping her head around to seek out the source of the voice, Jasmine was relieved to see that it was coming from the front of the line. Without hesitation, she abandoned Chris and quickly headed toward Eric, a member of the basketball team. "Hey babe, how are you doing?" she asked before straining to give him a kiss on the cheek. At five feet five, Jasmine had to stand on the tips of her toes to reach Eric, who was six feet four inches tall. She noticed the stunned expression on his face as he pulled away from her, and knew then that she had succeeded at her mission. Sure enough, Eric offered her a place next to him in line.

"Can you save at least one dance in there for me?"

"Of course I will. Thanks to you, I'll get in a lot quicker than I would had I stayed back there," said Jasmine, nodding toward the sour faces near the end of the line. Once the two of them finally made it to the gentleman who was accepting money for admission, Jasmine began unzipping her purse to retrieve her wallet, but Eric stopped her.

"Don't worry, Jazz. I got you."

"Aw, how sweet," she purred, caressing his chin with her hand.

"It's the least I can do for you, sweetheart."

The girl behind them folded her arms and sucked her teeth in disgust, but Jasmine paid her no mind. She figured that if the girl had any sense, she would learn how to play the game too, for she had painfully discovered long ago that guys certainly had no problems playing games with girls.

After flashing her I.D. to the gentleman who was guarding the door, Jasmine daintily held out her wrist so that he could slide on the red paper bracelet that she believed granted guests in-and-out privileges. As soon as she'd been validated, she took off toward the bar, leaving poor Eric behind. *Sorry babe, but tonight is Stacey's night.*

Immediately engulfed by a sea of people once she made it onto the dance floor, Jasmine struggled to make her way toward the back of the room where the bar was located. She was forced to push and fight her way past girls in tight pants, short skirts, and barely-there tops, as they shook every moveable part of their bodies, while guys in jeans, wife beaters, and fraternity coats grinded up against them. Bumping and grinding wasn't her style. Responding to cat calls, hisses, or guys who tugged on girls' arms instead of having the decency to look them in the eye and ask for a dance wasn't her style either. Jasmine didn't consider herself to be a "hoochie," a "hoe," or anyone's "baby." She was a lady, and expected to be treated as such.

"Let me get a Midori Sour!" Jasmine yelled at the bartender once she finally made it past the sea of music video wannabes. The DJ was playing music at ear-busting decibels, and the base could be felt vibrating through one's chest. The bartender therefore had to lean forward in order to hear her.

"Sure, anything for you, miss," replied the bartender with a wink. "I'll just need to see some I.D. first."

Jasmine was a little taken aback by the bartender's request, for she and half the people at the party were underage, but since when had that stopped bartenders from serving drinks to underage college students? Believing she could charm her way out of this little conundrum, Jasmine batted her eyelashes, smiled sweetly, then said, "Look, you and I both know that half the people you've served tonight have shown you their doctored I.D.'s. I wouldn't dare try to insult your intelligence by doing the same, so why don't you fix me that drink and I'll ask the DJ to play something slow for us during your break."

The bartender took a step back and looked Jasmine up and down before responding. "That offer sounds very tempting," he began, still scanning her frame. "But, I have a fiancé that wouldn't be too pleased if I were to take you up on it. Besides, I now see that cute little red bracelet on your wrist, which indicates that your age has already been verified, so please spare yourself further embarrassment and step aside so that I can serve the guests that are of age."

Angered by the bartender's response, Jasmine whipped her body around to face the dance floor. No sooner than she folded her arms across her chest in frustration, the deep, familiar cackle of Jackson Taylor could be heard coming from the far corner of the bar. With his back to her, Jasmine hadn't noticed Jackson when she first approached, and was upset to find that he was now getting a good laugh at her expense.

"You really are something, you know that?" stated Jackson, shaking his head and laughing. "You never cease to amaze me."

"Yeah, well, you never cease to annoy me," Jasmine replied, embarrassed and angry, all at the same time. She surveyed the dance floor, desperately trying to locate Stacey without having to walk through the dreaded sea of sweaty bodies again.

"See, this is why we need to be friends. If you're nice to me, I'll buy you that drink."

With his thick facial hair neatly groomed into a goatee, Jackson looked his age, and could have easily bought Jasmine any drink she desired without proof of I.D. However, she wasn't that desperate, for she had already been advised via campus gossip that Jackson wasn't the kind of man you accepted anything from, unless you planned on laying in his bed that same night. Ignoring his remark, Jasmine continued to look out into the crowd, hoping to spy some sign of Stacey. Although it was difficult to see inside the dimly lit room, she searched hard for the one reason she had come out that night.

"Why is it that whenever I talk to you, you seem distracted? As beautiful as you are, you shouldn't have to seek attention the way that you do."

"Excuse me?" she asked, feeling annoyed yet again, by Jackson's intrusion into her life. "Is there a point to this conversation?"

"The point is, how long are you going to play hard to get? I'm not asking you to marry me. Just dinner and a stroll along the beach would be nice. Do you realize how many of these ladies would rather partake in a nice evening out with a gentleman like me, than go on some sleazy trip to McDonalds, possibly a movie, and then back to the dorms with one of these chain wearing, grill sporting boys?" Jackson pointed to the dance floor where some guy, who had his hands firmly positioned on some girl's rear end, was grimacing with each pelvic thrust, while exposing his gold plated teeth to the crowd.

Jackson was right in that the demeanor and approach of his younger counterparts paled in comparison to his mature style and flair. There he was at a college party, wearing a dark suit and tie, while the majority of the men, or boys rather, had on wife beaters, and some no shirt at all, although security eventually made sure to reprimand those trying to audition for a Calvin Klein ad. The disparity was quite apparent, but Jasmine wasn't about to give Jackson any satisfaction by granting him such a compliment. He seemed to get a kick out of teasing her, so she definitely didn't have any kind words to throw in his direction.

"Gentleman?" she asked with one eyebrow raised. "Please. You are no gentleman."

"And you are no lady."

Infuriated, Jasmine stormed off in the direction in which she came. She decided that she'd much rather fight through the sea of musty bodies than deal with Jackson Taylor any longer. Her dismissal proved to be very timely, for she spotted Stacey entering the party as soon as she made it back toward the front of the room.

Stacey definitely knew how to stand out in a crowd. With his tan colored slacks, silky dress shirt and dress shoes, Stacey resembled a high fashion model. Elated by his presence, Jasmine hastened her steps as she headed toward the door to greet him. "Stacey!" she shouted, while waving one hand in the air so that he could see her. Yet, the music was so loud and the room so dim that he couldn't hear or see her. Instead, he remained near the door, and looked out as though he were waiting on someone.

"Stacey!" Jasmine yelled his name again, hoping that this time he would hear her, but he didn't. Feeling her heart skip a beat, Jasmine watched as Stacey turned to lend his arm to the person he had been waiting for at the door: Angel Martin…his date.

Angel noticed Jasmine before she could get Stacey's attention and beckoned for her to join them near the door. Taking a deep breath, Jasmine slowly walked toward them, using every fiber of her being to hold back her disappointment…and anger.

"What's up, Jasmine? Good to see you again!"

"You too, Angel," she replied, lying.

"Hi Jasmine. How are you doing?" asked Stacey.

Jasmine? Stacey usually addressed Jasmine by her nickname, "Jazz," yet suddenly found the need to be formal. Jasmine felt slighted and didn't understand why Stacey was putting up a front for Angel, a girl she thought bore no significance in his life. Although she had been introduced to Angel some time ago, Jasmine hadn't given her much thought considering that she didn't even go to Cal. Angel attended a junior college in Oakland, not too far from Berkeley. Despite the fact that she had seen her around campus with Stacey a few times after their initial encounter, Jasmine never thought much about her. For one, she didn't think Stacey could possibly be interested in a serious relationship with Angel, who she perceived as less attractive, less ambitious, and less outgoing than herself. In fact, she didn't really know what Stacey saw in her, aside from the fact that they were both interested in careers in education—Angel wanted to be an elementary school teacher and Stacey, dean of a college like his father someday.

"I'm fine," Jasmine finally replied to Stacey, who now had his arm wrapped around Angel's waist. She had to struggle to keep her blood from boiling. "So, Angel, what brings you here tonight? I didn't think a party like this was your scene." Angel was known for being such a goody-two-shoes that Jasmine couldn't picture her dancing alongside the men and women who were bumping and grinding like it was nobody's business just a few short feet away from where they were standing.

"Stacey really wanted to get out and unwind. He needs me by his side to make sure he doesn't get too crazy," she replied, giggling softly before playfully nudging Stacey's side with her elbow. Stacey looked down lovingly at her round, sweet face, which further angered Jasmine.

He's supposed to be looking at me like that!

Feeling like a deflated third wheel, Jasmine decided to excuse herself so that Stacey and Angel could be left alone to occupy the tiny bubble they had created for themselves. "I'm going to head over to the little girl's room, but it's good seeing you again, Angel, it really is," said Jasmine with a hint of sarcasm in her voice. She walked away and rolled her eyes as soon as her back was to them.

Clutching her purse so hard that her knuckles became sore, Jasmine marched out of the ballroom where the party was taking place and headed down the hall toward the ladies room. Once inside, she leaned up against the door to catch her breath. "This is not how this night was supposed to go down," she said to herself before entering an empty stall near the back of the room.

No sooner than she closed the door behind her, Jasmine heard some loud, obnoxious ladies enter the bathroom. One of them mentioned her name and suddenly gained her undivided attention.

The first girl: "Did you see Jasmine tonight?"

The second girl: "Yeah, I saw that bitch."

The first girl: "But did you see the way she weaseled her way to the front of the line and even got poor Eric Johnson to pay for her ticket?"

The second girl: "No, I missed that."

The third girl: "Well, Keisha and I both saw that. That girl is a trip."

The second girl: "She sure is."

The third girl: "Her dress is tight though."

The second girl: "You wouldn't think that if you saw how she was flirting with your man a few days ago."

The third girl: "David?"

The second girl: "Yes, David. She was all up in his grill at Café Milano."

No I wasn't! David approached me and asked if he could carry my books, to which I quickly replied, "No." I wasn't thinking about him—I was looking for Stacey!

The third girl: "Hmm. Well, her dress is tight, but she's not all that. If she was, she would be with Stacey. It's pathetic the way she follows him around campus like a little puppy dog. Unlike most of the guys here, he pays her no mind. Besides, I'm sure he'd much rather be with a sweet girl like Angel than a hoe like her."

Jasmine tried hard to fight back tears, but one escaped her grasp and rolled down her cheek. Listening to the petty gossip of her peers made her feel like she had suddenly been thrust back into high school. *Does Stacey really think I'm coming on too strong? Perhaps Missy is right.*

Wiping tears from her eyes, Jasmine immediately felt her pain transform into anger. *Who does Stacey think he is?* Most of the guys at Cal would have jumped at the chance to go out with her, which is why she was stumped by Stacey's odd behavior. She knew that he liked her, but didn't understand why he was dragging his feet when it came to advancing their relationship. Just look at Jackson, the new man on campus. He had been pursuing her relentlessly since he got there, and she hadn't given him the time of day.

Opening the stall door slowly, Jasmine made sure that the ladies had left the restroom before fully emerging. Her ears and cheeks grew warm as she approached the sink and stared hard at her reflection in the mirror. She began reapplying powder to cover up her tear-stained cheek, and although she fought hard to dismiss the ladies' hurtful words, she couldn't help but think of how stupid she'd been. *How dare Stacey play me for a fool!*

Not wanting to spend the rest of the evening watching Stacey prance around with Angel on his arm, Jasmine exited the ladies room and headed back toward the lobby of the hotel. Just when she decided to call it a night, she spied Stacey heading down the hallway towards the men's room, and a flood of emotions instantly poured over her. She hurried back toward the restrooms, hoping to steal just a few minutes of his time, which she thought would be all she needed to convince him he was making a terrible mistake.

"Stacey!" Jasmine yelled in a desperate attempt to catch him before he entered the men's room. Her breathing grew heavy as she rushed to catch up to him, one stiletto quickly passing in front of the other. "I was hoping I could talk to you alone, in private."

"Is everything Okay?" Stacey looked at Jasmine with concern and suddenly, she began to feel a strong, burning sensation build in the pit of her stomach.

Maybe I should just fall back like Missy said and let him approach me when he's ready. "Yeah, everything's fine," she said, ignoring her gut feeling to relent. "I just wanted to talk to you, like, for a sec."

Stacey's broad shoulders, which were once hunched up and tense, slowly eased back down as he fell into a relaxed pose. He smiled that gorgeous smile Jasmine had fallen in love with a year prior and said,

"Sure Jazz, let's go over here." Placing one hand on her arm, Stacey guided Jasmine back down the hallway towards the lobby.

The lobby was bustling with college students who had just arrived for the party and patrons who were checking in for the night. Stacy and Jasmine surveyed the area in search of a place where they could escape the crowd and talk in private. "Over there," Stacey said, pointing in the direction of one of the hotel's conference rooms. He maintained a light grip on Jasmine's arm as they walked side by side toward their destination. The warmth of his touch against the back of her arm was a feeling she wished could last forever...

Once they made it inside the conference room, which appeared to be unoccupied, Jasmine secured the door behind them to prevent anyone else from entering. This was the moment she'd long been waiting for, and wouldn't dare allow anyone to ruin it.

Chapter 5

"So, what's up?"

"Well, I wanted to talk to you about me...you...us."

Jasmine's heart pounded like it was preparing to rip through her chest. She craved a cigarette now more than ever.

"Oh," replied Stacey with an awkward grin. Blood rushed to his cheeks and Jasmine caught a slight glimpse of his dimples.

"I think you already know how I feel about you," she said, her stomach turning in knots. "I think you feel the same way about me, but we haven't allowed ourselves to see where our feelings can take us."

"Jasmine—"

"Wait," she pleaded, holding up a perfectly manicured hand. "Let me finish, please." Finally having built up the courage to speak her mind, Jasmine found Stacey's interruptions extremely annoying. She proceeded to talk over him like a bulldozer plowing through a wheat field. "It's just, well, you're not like any of the other guys on campus, and I know I'm not like most of the ladies around here, and...well, I think we would make a great team."

"Jazz, you know I'm with Angel."

"So."

"So?" Stacey's expression was an odd mixture of humor and disbelief. Jasmine averted her eyes from his and almost felt like running out of the room. Yet, before she could move her feet, Stacey took a step forward and placed one hand on her cheek. "Look, Jazz, you're a beautiful, intelligent young woman. I'm sure there are plenty of guys…" He hesitated, and Jasmine could feel her heart melting. "No," he continued, "I *know* there are plenty of guys who are dying to get with you."

"And you're not?" Suddenly, Jasmine's anxiety and nervousness was replaced with anger. "Stacey, why Angel?"

"Angel has a great heart and she and I share a lot of the same goals—"

"But you and I share the same drive. We both go after what we want and are successful at the things we pursue. Don't you see what a terrible mistake you're making?"

"Jazz, you're out of line."

"No, you're out of line!" Having lost her composure, tears welled up in the corners of her eyes. "Why did you lead me on then, huh? You didn't seem to think we weren't compatible all those times we hung out and you flirted with me!"

"*I* flirted with *you?*" Stacey took a step back and Jasmine watched as his shoulders became tense again. He looked shocked and angry, like she had just accused him of a crime he was completely innocent of committing. Yet, study dates at coffee shops, lunch breaks shared at Pleasant Beginnings, friendly emails and playful winks all came to mind, thus confirming her assertion. Jasmine knew she hadn't imagined things, but it was clear that Stacey wasn't quite ready to fess up. "So, it's all *my* fault, huh?" he persisted. "You flirt with *everyone*, Jazz!"

Jasmine should have braced herself, because she wasn't prepared to handle what Stacey said. The moment he spoke those last words, something inexplicable took hold of her, and she had no control over what happened next. All she knew was that her hand started flying through the air, and a few seconds later, Stacey was rubbing the left side of his face, which was bright red and undoubtedly stinging from the pain her palm left after connecting with his cheek.

Shaking his head in disgust, Stacey gave Jasmine one last look before heading out the door. Jasmine was left alone in the conference room with tears streaming down her face. She had never felt more humiliated in her entire life.

Chapter 6

Jasmine stood in the middle of the conference room, stunned by Stacey's words, as she desperately attempted to pull herself together before heading out into the lobby. She could hear the hustle and bustle of patrons behind her and had absolutely no idea how she was going to walk out and face everyone. *How could he?* she asked herself before wiping the tears from her face. She felt herself grow hotter with each passing moment, for she couldn't escape Stacey's words, or the venom that was spewed by the women in the bathroom. *Who do they think they are?* The angrier she became, the hotter she felt, until finally she couldn't take it anymore.

Violently grabbing hold of her purse, Jasmine reached back as far as her arm would go. All the anger and pain that had built up inside of her was now being used as fuel to hurl her purse across the room. The purse hit the wall in front of her and bounced back before crashing to the floor, just as she let out a cry of frustration. She barely had a chance to place her arm back at her side before noticing an image emerge from the shadows in the far corner of the room.

"Whoa, take it easy. You might need that later."

"Jackson? But...I, I thought this room was empty."

"I had just come in to admire the beautiful painting on the wall when you and Stacey barged in. I ducked over here, in this corner—"

"So you could spy on us?"

"Spy on you? I was in here first."

"So! You could have said something when you saw us come in here! What is your problem?" asked Jasmine, furious and embarrassed, all at the same time.

"I don't have a problem. I was just enjoying the décor, and, well, a lot more." He looked Jasmine up and down, which caused her to feel nauseous.

"So, you heard everything, huh?"

"Pretty much," Jackson replied, letting out a soft chuckle as he approached. "You two ran in here as if the building was on fire, so my instincts told me to hide in the corner. I thought it would keep me safe from the flames, but apparently not."

"Is that supposed to be funny?"

"Maybe. I guess you can say I was curious to see how a softie like Stacey would handle a woman like you. Most men can't handle aggressive women, and he crumbled, just like I thought he would."

"Who are you, Jackson? Why is my life of such interest to you?"

"Please, don't flatter yourself. I think you've done enough of that for one night."

Seeing that there was no getting through to a rude, cocky man like Jackson, Jasmine whizzed past him to retrieve her purse before storming out the conference room. Jackson, she was sure, was greatly amused by everything he witnessed that night. She found him to be tactless and feared he would run off and tell others about her encounter with Stacey. Everyone on campus would be laughing at her next semester, just like the ladies in the bathroom.

Jackson mumbled something under his breath as she exited, but Jasmine was too busy fuming to care. Besides, she had nothing else to say to him. In fact, she hoped to never speak to Jackson Taylor again.

Chapter 7

Despite her run in with Stacey, Jasmine still had feelings for him—feelings that just wouldn't seem to go away. She meant everything she said to him about being different from other guys, for Stacey was more than just a cute face and nice body; he had the ability to make time stop whenever she was with him. School, issues with catty women—nothing mattered to Jasmine when Stacey was around. Just seeing him brought a smile to her face and turned an otherwise mundane day into an exciting one. Hearing his voice sent butterflies fluttering in her stomach, and his touch—even just a handshake sent chills down her spine. She hadn't felt that way about anyone in a long time.

Jasmine hadn't developed real feelings for anyone since Demetri, whom she had met while a sophomore in high school. Although he was fine, charming, and considered to be one of the cool kids on campus, she didn't really know what to think of him at first because the concept of love and sex eluded her. Having lost her mother to a car accident at the age of five, Jasmine didn't have anyone to turn to for guidance concerning womanhood. She tried to turn to her father, but he immediately shut down emotionally due to an inability to cope with the pain. Thus, she remained guarded when it came to relationships…that is of course until some of Demetri's charm began to slowly chip away at her resolve.

After a year of wooing, Jasmine finally caved in to Demetri's advances and agreed to become his girlfriend. He appeared to genuinely care for her, and slowly began opening up about some of the issues he had to deal with at home, which in turn made Jasmine feel comfortable confiding in him about some of her deepest thoughts and feelings. Demetri was the first person she ever spoke to truthfully about her mother's passing. Prior to that she had simply told others that she was too young to remember anything about her mother, when in reality she had faint, yet fond memories of the woman who sang silly lullabies to her at night to help her go to sleep, and constantly told her how beautiful and smart she was. Demetri listened to Jasmine and gave her a shoulder to cry on—one that her father couldn't even provide. As a result, she drew closer to him and began showering him with gifts, yet was unfortunately too young and naïve to realize that Demetri had actually succeeded in seducing her.

Jasmine lost her virginity to Demetri, and what should have been a private and pleasant experience turned into a nightmare once he made it a point to tell his friends and anyone who would listen how he had finally "nailed" the prettiest girl in school. She was devastated, and to add insult to injury, her so-called friends turned on her, further fueling the gossip that sought to mar her reputation. What started out as a story of how she had "given it up" to her boyfriend, further escalated into a tale of how she had slept with most of the boys in the student body.

Hurt and betrayed, Jasmine dealt with her heartache the only way she knew how: avoidance. Whereas most kids spent their last year of high school partying and preparing for the prom, Jasmine stayed holed up in her bedroom and counted the days to graduation. Although she had gotten accepted to UCLA and USC, she decided to attend Cal to further distance herself from it all. There was nothing left for her in

L.A. as far as she was concerned, aside from her father of course, but he had his own life and it was time she started living hers.

With a fresh start in a new atmosphere, Jasmine was ready to take on life with a new attitude. Although she had dated since Demetri, she never allowed any relationship to last longer than a season, for she knew that the more time that passed, the more at risk she was at falling in love and ending up heartbroken again. She definitely didn't want to get hurt, but couldn't resist the yearning for companionship. Without her father or any girlfriends close by, Jasmine really was all alone. Stacey was therefore the only boy she had given serious thought to since Demetri, and for some reason couldn't shake her infatuation for him.

Aside from him being smart and good looking, Stacey stood out from other guys because he wasn't trying to be a player, and was extremely ambitious with a good head on his shoulders. Plus, he wasn't pursuing Jasmine like most of the young men she encountered, which she found truly refreshing. What should have felt like rejection actually made Jasmine feel safe, for Stacey didn't seem to have any hidden agendas like most of the guys she knew. His aloofness made her desire him more, and she wanted to be wherever he was, and do whatever he was doing…which is exactly why she decided to call her father and tell him that she'd be staying in the Bay Area for the summer after all.

Although she didn't need any additional credits, Jasmine signed up for a few courses on Shakespeare to convince her father that she was trying to boost her intellect and actually had a reason to stay on campus. Besides, what was there for her to do in L.A. except shop and hang out with her family? True, she missed her father and relatives, but home just held too many painful memories that she had no interest in revisiting.

"Jasmine. Jasmine!"

"Yes."

"Girl, don't you hear me talking to you? Pass me the remote control now so I can watch my stories."

"Sure. Sorry." Jasmine had zoned out while thinking about Stacey as she stared through the window of Missy's room. In addition to taking summer courses, she had also decided to put in extra hours volunteering at the assisted living facility. Missy, who was still bedridden since her stroke some months prior, was thrilled to have her. She hated having random people come in and out of her room and was relieved to know that Jasmine would be with her consistently throughout the year. Her presence helped put her mind at ease, probably more than Jasmine would ever know.

"Is everything okay? You seem awful quiet."

"Yeah, everything's fine…I guess. Well, it's just that—"

"Hush now, my stories are on."

Jasmine sat down at the foot of Missy's bed and gazed up at the plasma television that was suspended from the wall just a few feet above them. It was good that Missy told her to be quiet, for how could she ever explain to her what a fool she had made of herself, chasing after Stacey the way that she did? She had done exactly what Missy told her not to do. Besides, Missy never approved of her liking Stacey to begin with.

Missy liked Stacey, but didn't like the fact that he appeared to be less interested in Jasmine than she was in him. She couldn't hate on him too much though because it was he who had introduced her to Jasmine. Stacey started volunteering at Pleasant Beginnings a few weeks before Jasmine did, and although he had been assigned to care for someone else, he checked in on Missy from time to time. They developed somewhat of a rapport, so even though he quit volunteering shortly after her stroke, he'd since been in to check on her. Although she appreciated the sentiment, it seemed Missy found any mention of Stacey by Jasmine to be quite annoying.

Missy may have thought that Jasmine was simply chasing after Stacey, but she didn't know the truth behind their relationship. Stacey liked Jasmine, and for a short period of time had entertained the thought of pursuing a relationship with her. Yet, he hadn't done it in the most honest way, which inadvertently succeeded at getting Jasmine's hopes up. It all started with "innocent" lunch dates between classes and breaks at Pleasant Beginnings, which soon escalated into the exchange of friendly emails. Jasmine should have found it odd that Stacey never asked for her phone number or gave her his, but instead of heeding this pertinent warning sign, she chose to ignore it because they shared a few classes and volunteered together, which therefore made it easy for her to get in contact with him. Stacey definitely never had a problem connecting with Jasmine via email, like he had on the afternoon of their first "date." It all started when she received the following message in her inbox: WHAT'S UP JAZZ? I HAVE A SHIFT TONIGHT THAT WRAPS AT 8:00, AND YOU? HOPE TO SEE YOU LATER. --STACEY

Jasmine was so excited behind Stacey's email that she didn't even respond. Instead, she waited to talk to him face to face, hunting him down at the facility during their break in her typical, brazen fashion. "Hey, I got your email. What's up?"

"What's up with you?" Stacey replied as he held out his arms. She eagerly responded by wrapping her arms around his neck.

"I get off at 8:15."

"Cool. If you wanna hang out later I can stick around for a few and wait for you."

"Sure," Jasmine replied, feeling like she had just been hurled into outer space. She danced through her shift the rest of the evening and got on Missy's nerves for being so jittery. As soon as her time was up, she kissed Missy goodnight and darted down the hallway to where Stacey was waiting.

"Wanna go to Yogurt Park for dessert?" he asked.

"Sounds good to me," replied Jasmine enthusiastically. She would have agreed to eat sawdust with him.

The two of them decided to take a stroll through campus while they devoured their frozen yogurt. It was the first time they had a chance to truly be alone, for it was just him, her, and the stars above. Jasmine took notice of how clear the sky was that night, as she observed the little dipper, which sat directly above them as they approached the Campanile. As they became engaged in a deep conversation about life and their plans for the future, Jasmine couldn't help but feel that the stars were aligned as a sign that her dreams were about to come true.

"What do you want to do after you graduate?"

"I want to go to law school, but would love to take some time off to travel."

"Yeah, same here. I mean, I definitely plan to go to grad school to get my master's so that I can teach on the college level, but I'd first like to visit Spain. I hear it's gorgeous there. I also want to go to Greece."

"Me too!" Jasmine replied, staring at Stacey incredulously. They truly shared a lot of the same interests, and Jasmine was intrigued by Stacey's drive. "So, you don't wanna turn pro?"

"Football's cool, but it's not something I can do for the rest of my life. Even if I were to go pro, I'd probably only be able to do it for a good ten years or so, tops. Besides, my heart just isn't in it as a career. I mean, don't get me wrong, I love football, and I'm proud of all that I've accomplished. Yet, I really am passionate about teaching, and that's what I really want to do."

"I respect that," Jasmine replied. "It's rare that people pursue their true passion in life. A lot of folks chase money, but I've learned there are a lot more important things in life…and things that can bring you more joy than money."

Stacey listened intently to everything Jasmine said. It were as if he truly felt a connection with her, for they locked eyes at that moment and remained silent. He then placed one hand against the curve of her waist and the other on the left side of her jaw before drawing her in close. He pressed his lips firmly against hers as they shared a brief, yet intense kiss, then abruptly pulled away and apologized for being so forward.

The kiss was the first bold move Stacey had ever made, and it sent Jasmine's head spinning. She assured him that he had absolutely nothing to apologize for, yet he continued to express how sorry he was, then told her he was taking her home. Jasmine didn't know what to make of Stacey's apologetic tone after they kissed…that is of course, not until she found out about Angel. Stacey obviously felt conflicted since he was with Angel, but had feelings for Jasmine. Jasmine of course found his supposed relationship with Angel silly, and didn't understand what the big deal was. Yet, it proved to be a big deal to Stacey, who after their "date," went through a phase where he could barely look Jasmine in the eye. The winks and flirtatious glances stopped, as did the emails, lunch dates, and coffee house chatter. Before long, Stacey quit volunteering at Pleasant Beginnings, so Jasmine couldn't even see him at work. He eventually eased up and started talking to her again, but things hadn't been quite the same between them since that night.

Jasmine couldn't tell Missy about her encounter with Stacey at the hotel, just as she couldn't bring herself to tell her about their night out some months prior, because she wouldn't understand and would probably think it sounded cheap: a kiss outside with a boy at night, and it wasn't even a real date. Her knowing that definitely wouldn't change how she already felt about him. Yet, as far as Jasmine was concerned, Missy didn't understand a lot of things when it came to relationships because she was the same person who had told her it was high time she move on and forgive Demetri. Forgiving Demetri would mean that Jasmine would have to take responsibility for her own decisions, which was a hard pill to swallow. It was much easier to place the blame on someone else, so she simply accepted the fact that she had been a fool once, and was determined to not be a fool twice.

Chapter 8

Summer didn't go as Jasmine planned because her father was right about Stacey going away to football camp. She therefore didn't see any sign of him the entire time she was in the Bay Area. Yet, she figured it was for the best, as she hoped the break would provide Stacey enough time to forget about their little episode in the conference room at the hotel. After all, she wanted a fresh start and an opportunity to redeem herself.

Luckily, Jasmine didn't see Jackson around campus either. He was from Las Vegas, and word around town was that his family owned a casino out there. She didn't know if that were true or not, but that would definitely have explained a lot about the man who wore nice suits to parties and drove an incredibly expensive car. Yet, none of that mattered to her of course because she was too busy focusing on how to get another shot with Stacey.

Jasmine aced her Shakespeare courses and actually enjoyed learning about Romeo and Juliet for the millionth time. Before meeting Stacey she found the whole love at first sight thing ridiculous, but now saw the two of them as a modern day Romeo and Juliet. However, instead of there being feuding families to keep them apart, Jasmine saw

Angel as the only thing standing in the way of her obtaining true love and happiness.

After renting a car for a week during the summer in order to "explore the Bay Area better," Jasmine bumped into Angel while in Oakland one hot afternoon. She pretended to pay a visit to Merritt College to check out the summer programs they offered, but was actually going to spy out the competition. *Just what is so special about Angel anyway?*

After spending a few hours with Missy at the assisted living facility, Jasmine made sure to change out of her uniform and into some of her usual, stylish clothes before heading out to Oakland. If she were going to see Angel, she definitely wasn't going to do so in that ugly frock of a gown they forced her to wear to keep from "distracting the residents." Donning a flattering pair of low-rise blue jeans, a teal crop top that accentuated her well-defined midsection, and a pair of teal platform wedge heels, Jasmine slipped on a pair of her freshest stunner shades before exiting the facility to face the beautiful summer day.

Jasmine allowed the wind to whip through her long locks as she drove around Oakland in the drop-top convertible she talked her father into renting for her. She had never been to the Merritt College campus before and therefore had no idea where to look for Angel, but was certain she would easily be able to spot her because people always talked about what a strong presence she was not only on campus, but in the community as well. Angel was known for her volunteer efforts, such as working at local elementary schools, the Children's Hospital, and on campus in the Recruitment and Retention Center. Thus, with the numerous summer programs in existence that were geared toward prospective college students, Jasmine knew she was bound to see Angel somewhere, doing something.

Sure enough, Jasmine spotted Angel standing near a grassy knoll, talking to a group of teenagers just moments after stepping foot on the Merritt College campus. Feeling nervous and anxious, she reached inside her purse to pull out a pack of cigs she had started working on earlier in the week. Times like this called for a stress reliever, which she tended to find at the filtered end of a burning cigarette. After taking a long drag, her muscles seemed to relax and the tension inside her stomach subsided. Two puffs later, she felt stable enough to proceed.

Angel didn't spot Jasmine right away, which enabled her to stand back and watch her rival in action. The teens seemed to be very attentive as they listened to Angel babble on about the history of the campus and the programs it had to offer. Jasmine took notice of how well she enunciated each word perfectly, and had to admit that even in a sloppy T-shirt and jeans, Angel was well poised. With her auburn colored hair slicked back into a low hanging ponytail and minimal makeup on her face, Angel was a simple beauty who exuded an air of confidence well beyond her years.

Watching Angel engage with the teens outside near the grassy knoll made Jasmine think back to the night she and Stacey shared a kiss underneath the stars. A smirk slowly crept across her face as she reminisced about that night, and continued to intensify almost uncontrollably, as she began to fantasize about all the other moments she dreamt of sharing with Stacey.

"…And that concludes this portion of our tour." Suddenly, Jasmine found herself thrust back into reality once she heard Angel begin to wrap up her speech. "If there are no more questions, I would like for each of you to head over to the student union where food and beverages are being served."

Jasmine wanted to head back to her car before Angel spied her lingering in the background, but before she could slip away, one of the boys in the group turned around and took notice of her standing a few feet behind. "Daaamn!" he exclaimed. "If this is what the women look like here, I'm definitely enrolling!" Stopping dead in her tracks, Jasmine turned around to face Angel and the group of teens, who had their eyes directly focused on her.

"Jasmine? Is that you?"

"Yeah, it's me."

Grinning a thousand-watt smile, Angel gave Jasmine a warm greeting, indicating her lack of awareness in the matter concerning Stacey and the embarrassing incident she had with him the night of the party. Breathing a sigh of relief, Jasmine proceeded to head toward Angel, who beckoned for her to approach.

"What a surprise seeing you here! How's it going?" she asked, as the teens began to disperse.

"Good," Jasmine replied, shifting her weight uncomfortably onto one leg.

"What are you doing here? I've never seen you around here before."

"Do you own this campus?" is what Jasmine wanted to say, but instead she slowly lifted her shades and allowed them to rest on top of her forehead before politely responding. "Oh, I was just on my way to the nail salon and thought I'd stop by and check out the library here. I'm taking some Shakespeare courses this summer and thought I'd see what Merritt's library has to offer."

"Shakespeare for the summer? That's cool! I love Shakespeare! But, Cal has an excellent library. I would think that between theirs and the downtown Berkeley Public Library you'd be able to find everything you need," Angel replied, looking puzzled.

Jasmine simply ignored Angel's incredulous stare and asked, "So, how's Stacey? I haven't seen him around lately." She searched her face for some sign, some indication that Stacey had told her something about what happened the night of the party, but there was none.

"Stacey's cool. He's just busy with football practice, as usual. I'll probably hear from him tonight."

"Oh," said Jasmine, feeling slightly relieved yet annoyed by Angel's cool demeanor. A small part of her wished Stacey had said something about the incident to Angel. Did he find her that insignificant to not even have mentioned her in a conversation? Feeling that her investigation was going nowhere, Jasmine decided to put an end to her visit, but Angel stopped her from leaving. "Well, I guess I'll let you get back to what you were doing—"

"Oh no, you're not bothering me at all. In fact, we could use some more help around here."

"Help?"

"Yeah. We're about to serve lunch to the teens and could use some extra help in the kitchen. The faster we get them fed, the faster we can get on with the rest of the tours."

"Well, I dunno. I mean, I gotta…"

"Come on," said Angel, grabbing Jasmine by the arm. She dragged her across campus as they headed toward the student union, where a bunch of teens and their campus guides had gathered. She wasted no time putting Jasmine to work, as she directed her towards the back of the room where the kitchen was located. "Here, just put these on and get in line," she said before handing her a hairnet and a pair of plastic gloves. There were about four other young ladies in the kitchen, frantically shoveling food that had just come out of the oven onto platters that were being escorted out to where the mass of hungry college prospects were waiting.

It was summertime, and the weather was scorching hot outside, so the last place Jasmine or anyone wanted to be was in the back of some steaming hot kitchen, serving food to ungrateful teenagers. The ladies in the kitchen could sense Jasmine's uneasiness and began glaring at her with disdain, as if to telepathically inquire, "Who does she think she is?" Aware of the daggers being tossed in her direction, Jasmine quickly piled her hair on top of her head before sliding on the hairnet and gloves.

"I'll be out there, serving food," said Angel, pointing outside the kitchen to where the hungry mob waited. "Don't worry, the ladies back here will take good care of you." Placing one hand on Jasmine's shoulder, Angel wished her luck before leaving her to fend for herself in the presence of the mean-mugging ladies, who continued to stare at her like they wanted to toss her inside the oven with the food.

When she had awakened that morning, Jasmine had no idea she'd be spending the rest of her day helping Angel in any way, let alone sweating in a hot college kitchen to serve food to a bunch of rowdy, college-bound kids. She was irritated and uncomfortable, yet noticed how Angel seemed to enjoy every minute of her volunteer duties. As she watched her go in and out of the kitchen, Jasmine could see the passion in Angel's face, for she truly wanted everything to run smoothly, and see every teen happy and fed.

The more Jasmine observed Angel act selflessly, the more it reminded her of how she had been back in high school. Although she didn't desire to go back to being "a chump," as she called it, Jasmine couldn't help but begin to understand what Stacey found appealing about Angel, who appeared to be genuinely sweet and caring.

Like Stacey, Angel didn't have an air of craftiness about her, which was refreshing and unique. She was smart, kind, considerate, and basically shared many of the same qualities Stacey seemed to possess. Jasmine knew Stacey was special when she first discovered he worked at Pleasant Beginnings, but apparently needed more of an opportunity to convince him that she was truly something special too.

Chapter 9

Fall finally arrived and Jasmine was happy because it marked the beginning of her third year at Cal. She had declared English as her major, thus moving one step closer toward graduating. She was also happy that summer was over because it meant she would get to see Stacey again, for she had spent most of the time wondering what he thought about her since the incident in the hotel conference room. Was he sorry about what he said? Did he go to bed with thoughts of her on his mind? Did he dream about her? Perhaps he finally realized he had made a terrible mistake and was finally ready to give them a chance. Since it was already the third week of school and she hadn't seen any sign of him on campus, Jasmine was on the verge of driving herself crazy thinking about the myriad of thoughts that could have possibly been running through his mind…

It was a Tuesday afternoon when Jasmine finally ran into Stacey for the first time since the spring. Desiring to squeeze in some physical activity before her next class, she headed down to the Recreational Sports Facility, otherwise known as the RSF, for a much needed workout. After blowing off steam in a kickboxing class, Jasmine was amazed by the amount of tension and anxiety she had allowed to build up inside of her over the whole Stacey fiasco. She had to admit that the adrenaline rush and subsequent sense of calm she felt after her workout was better than any sensation she'd ever gained from taking a drag on a cigarette. The moment she emerged from the locker room, freshly showered and groomed, is when she ran into Stacey, literally, in the gym lobby. "Hey, I've been looking for you."

Jasmine had been walking with her head tilted downward while she searched inside her duffel bag for her cell phone, so the sound of Stacey's voice startled her. Frazzled, she took a step back to keep from falling down from shock. With his hands firmly gripping her arms, Stacey helped Jasmine maintain her balance. "Whoa. You all right?" he asked, looking concerned.

"Yeah, yes," she replied, which was a lie. Jasmine was completely caught off guard, and to make matters worse, Stacey was standing in front of her wearing nothing but a pair of gray cotton shorts and sneakers. He and his teammates had already tired themselves out by jogging across campus to get to the gym, so tiny streams of sweat ran from his shoulders and down his well defined pecs, eventually making their way to his stomach, which looked more like an eight pack than a six. Jasmine was in such awe that she had to blink a few times to keep from getting lost in the moment. She struggled to regain her composure, but stumbled over her words, only appearing more uneasy. "Oh...hey...hi," she continued awkwardly. "You...you were looking for me?"

"Yeah," said Stacey. He paused for a moment, and Jasmine watched as his long, dark lashes fell over his beautiful, brown eyes, which looked soft, almost like a puppy dog's. Grinning nervously, he asked, "Things are cool between me and you, right?"

"Yeah," replied Jasmine with slight hesitation in her voice. She was pleasantly surprised by his question, for it implied that he had been thinking about her over the summer. Although she wasn't quite sure what he meant by "cool," she figured that if he were willing to put her dramatic outburst behind them, then things were definitely "cool" between them.

"Great," replied Stacey, who was now smiling from ear to ear. It was as if he too were relieved they had finally made amends.

Jasmine wanted to talk to Stacey longer and see where his head was at in terms of where their relationship was heading, but he cut the conversation short. "Well, you take care, okay? I've gotta run."

"Okay," said Jasmine, trying to play it cool. She watched Stacey walk away and felt herself growing anxious all over again. She almost couldn't believe he had taken the initiative to patch things up between them. If there was any doubt in her mind that there still existed a chance for them to be together, it was erased the moment she saw him look back at her and smile before rounding the corner to enter the weight room. No words could describe the happiness she felt at that moment.

****

Jasmine ended up running into Jackson for the first time since the party the same day she ran into Stacey. Things always seemed to work out that way: She'd be looking for Stacey, and Jackson wouldn't be too far behind, looking for her. After leaving the RSF, she made her way over to the Golden Bear Café to grab a bite to eat before heading off to her next class.

While standing in front of the refrigerated goods, Jasmine tried to decide if she wanted cold sushi, or a fresh sandwich prepared by one of the attendants behind the counter. Yet, before she could make up her mind, a soft tap landed on her shoulder, causing her to turn around.

"Hey beautiful, you miss me?"

Jackson stood before Jasmine, and she studied him for a moment, as she tried to decide whether or not to entertain him with a response. Yet, noticing the stubble on his face instantly inspired her to speak. "Didn't have time to shave, did we? Not a good look Jackson."

"Yeah, I know," he replied, rubbing his jaw. Jasmine should have known Jackson would have a comeback for her insult because he had a comeback for everything. "I was up all night thinking about how I haven't seen my Jasmine in a while, and, well, I guess I forgot to shave."

She hated to admit it, but even with an unkempt goatee, Jackson still looked good. Those deep, dark eyes of his were truly captivating, and she knew it was possible to get lost in them if she weren't careful.

"Well, I'd love to stay and chat, but I've gotta run," she said, quickly averting her eyes from his. Grabbing a packet of sushi from the refrigerator and a diet soda, Jasmine headed over to the cashier to pay for her items. She plopped her gym bag down on the counter and opened her purse to begin searching for her wallet, but before she could whip it out, Jackson stepped in front of her and handed the cashier a twenty dollar bill. Rolling her eyes in frustration, Jasmine didn't say a word. It was obvious there was no shaking this man.

As Jasmine scrambled to place her belongings back inside her purse, Jackson noticed the open pack of cigarettes peaking through the top, then reached inside and pulled them out. "Excuse you!" she huffed, enraged by the audacity of his action. She attempted to snatch the pack of cigarettes away from him, but he was much taller than she and simply dangled them over her head in a game of keep away.

"I didn't know you were a smoker?"

"Well, I'm sure there are plenty of things you don't know about me, Jackson."

"Wait a minute," he said before pausing to look down at the duffel bag draped across her shoulder. He observed the container of sushi he had just purchased for her, then scanned the pack of cigarettes in his hand. "Let me get this straight, you work out, eat healthy, and smoke? Real smart."

"First of all, it's none of your damn business what I do. Second of all, you can't talk to me about health considering you're about to devour that fat-laden cupcake," said Jasmine, looking down at the plastic, see-through container Jackson held in his other hand. "And for your information," she offered as her final comeback, "I don't smoke...I mean, I do smoke, but not often."

"I dated a smoker once, and it wasn't fun. I told myself I wouldn't date a smoker again, so I guess that means you have to quit."

"Don't count on it," Jasmine replied before grabbing her container of sushi and soda from the cashier. She headed out the door without giving Jackson another look.

Jasmine was irritated with Jackson and couldn't understand why she always seemed to allow him to get under her skin. Yet, as annoying as his intrusive behavior was, she still didn't allow it to overshadow the joy she felt from knowing that things were still "cool" between she and Stacey. In fact, she swore that no encounter with Jackson would ever make her stop thinking about Stacey...or his chiseled body...and those dimples.

Chapter 10

Although Jasmine felt like she had a real chance with Stacey again, she unfortunately didn't have much of an opportunity to pursue it considering that the semester was kicking her butt. She was taking courses within her English major and had discovered what every junior in college does sooner or later, which is that general education courses are nowhere near as tough as the classes required for one's major.

Freshman and sophomore year had been a breeze for Jasmine, who had gotten A's left and right with minimal effort. Now however, she was finding it extremely difficult to ace her classes, volunteer at the assisted living facility, and still have time and energy to party. She therefore didn't see much of Stacey, except in passing. They said "What's up" to each other, whenever they had the chance, and Stacey would ask Jasmine how Missy was doing, but that was about it. Jackson, on the other hand, would walk with Jasmine, or stalk her, as she put it, to and from her classes, and continued to pursue her as though she were a prize to be won.

The only exciting thing Jasmine had to look forward to that semester was the Big Game, which took place every year between Cal and Stanford. The Cal Bears had unfortunately lost to the Stanford Cardinal the previous year and were hoping to redeem themselves. Jasmine hated attending sporting events and only planned to do so to watch Stacey play. Yet, even she had to admit that the Big Game was like no other game.

It was an age-old tradition for the two local rivals to go toe to toe, so proud alumni from all parts of the globe would gather in late November or early December of each year to watch as Cal and Stanford battled for victory. There were pre and post-parties galore, and Mr. Fairchild planned to fly up so that he could attend the game with his daughter. Jasmine had purchased their tickets early because she knew they would sell out quickly, and sure enough, after the first few days of sales, the game was sold out.

In the midst of all her studying and volunteer work, Jasmine eagerly waited for game day to arrive. It was going to be the first time that year she'd be able to catch a break and truly enjoy some downtime. Plus, she was thrilled at the prospect of being able to spend some time with her father, who she hadn't seen all year. Yet, as was often the case, "something came up," thus preventing Mr. Fairchild from attending.

Mr. Fairchild called Jasmine and explained to her that he needed to stay in L.A. to take care of some important business. She was disappointed, but had grown accustomed to her father backing out of events that required them to spend quality time together. With the game less than a month away, Jasmine was stuck with an extra ticket, and although she could have easily scanned through the list of numbers in her cell phone to pick out a guy to go to the game with, she really didn't want to be bothered. Most of the guys she knew didn't truly want to be "just friends," so she knew that whoever she called would expect more out of the situation, when all she really wanted was a companion.

Selling the extra ticket wouldn't have been hard considering there'd be several scalpers and plenty of eager buyers on game day. Yet, the truth was that Jasmine didn't want to go to the game alone because rumors had begun circulating around campus about a possible riot that was to ensue if Cal didn't win. Supposedly, a group of students planned to rush the field and tear things up. Jasmine already felt uneasy about going to the game alone, so the last thing she needed was for something crazy like that to jump off.

Why sporting events were so important to people, Jasmine had no idea. She could definitely understand the concept of wanting to win, but the way spectators became so enraged when their team lost, or overjoyed when their team won was beyond her. The fans weren't the ones winning the prize, so she figured it was just one of those guy things that she would never understand. There was however one man who didn't understand it either, and that was Jackson.

"Look at how crazy they're acting," said Jackson, who sat next to Jasmine in the stands of the Hearst Greek Theater, the home of the infamous bonfire rally.

Each year, Cal threw a huge party known as the bonfire rally the night before the Big Game, where attendees young and old celebrated impending victory. Rituals were performed on stage before a huge bonfire that served to ignite team spirit, and some people would get so rowdy that the event became comical if nothing else. Although Jackson had no intention of attending the game, even he had decided to partake in the festivities. Jasmine was a little annoyed when she first noticed him emerge through the crowd of partygoers, but a small part of her had grown accustomed to him following her around. She therefore sat next to him and took in the sights while three shirtless, pot-bellied fans ran past them toward the bonfire.

With Cal colors painted on their faces and bodies, the three young men began shouting profanities and talking about how they were going to "murder" members of the opposing team. Although they weren't on the team and therefore wouldn't actually have the opportunity to go toe to toe with Stanford, they seemed to greatly enjoy acting as though they were.

"Crazy?" Jasmine inquired, while staring at Jackson's unbelievably clear, chocolate skin. He sat so close that even she was surprised that she was allowing him to be near her. In fact, it made her a little uncomfortable, so she decided to spark up their usual banter to relieve some of the tension. "What, are you jealous that you can't play?"

"Jealous? Jealous of what? Not being able to hug up on other men and get all muddy and sweaty with them?" Jackson looked at Jasmine with a sly grin, indicating that he was about to say something smart. "The fact that you would even be interested in a guy who enjoys hugging and squeezing other dudes is beyond me."

Jackson loved taking shots at Stacey, who Jasmine hadn't seen any sign of all night. She had attended the rally in hopes of catching him before the game to wish him luck. Unable to spot him in the crowd, she instead found herself chatting it up with Jackson to pass the time.

"Why are you going to the game if you hate the sport so much?"

"I'm not," Jackson replied. "My aunt, who lives in Richmond, asked me to take my cousin to the game. He plays high school football and she thought it would be good for him to see a college game. They're both upset though, 'cause it sold out before I could get tickets. I therefore decided to bring him here as a consolation."

No sooner than Jackson stopped talking, Jasmine looked over to her right and saw a young boy, who looked no older than fifteen, approach wearing a bulky jacket that was too large for his frame. He was carrying a bunch of snacks in his hands, but was so scrawny that he could barely hold on to the food that seemed to overwhelm his small grasp.

"Speak of the devil," said Jackson, who looked over at the kid and rolled his eyes.

The kid, who was clumsily heading in their direction, definitely looked like he was related to Jackson. With the same thick eyebrows and piercing dark eyes, Jackson and the kid could have easily been mistaken for brothers. However, it soon became apparent to Jasmine that everything can't be passed down through genetics, because the kid, who was gangly and about her height, not only lacked Jackson's stature, but his sense of style and grace as well.

Jasmine and Jackson watched as his cousin tripped over his own shoe, sending the meal bars and other treats he was carrying, flying through the air. The kid lunged forward in an attempt to save it all, and ended up looking like he was auditioning for a juggling act with the circus. "I sure hope he can handle a football better than he does those snacks."

"Be nice."

"Why, you're not," Jasmine replied before zipping up her black hooded sweater. She slid her hands inside her coat pockets because it was cold, and not clear out like it was the night she and Stacey kissed.

"Why didn't you leave some of that stuff in the car?" Jackson asked his cousin.

"Man, I told you I was going to eat all of this. You know I'm trying to beef up."

"Whatever," Jackson replied, looking annoyed. He then introduced his cousin to Jasmine. "Jamal, I want you to meet Jasmine. Jasmine, meet my cousin, Jamal."

"What's up?" asked Jasmine with her hands still stuffed inside her pockets. She had no intention of shaking the kid's hand, but he grabbed her arm anyway, pulling her hand out of her pocket. She thought he was just going to shake it, but the kid went a step further and kissed the back of it with his dry, crusty lips.

"It's a pleasure to make your acquaintance, pretty lady."

The kid was obviously a ham and desperately needed to practice his game if he ever wished for it to be as smooth as Jackson's. "Nice meeting you," Jasmine replied before wiping her hand on her sweater.

"So, you going to the game?" asked Jamal.

"Yeah. My father was supposed to fly up from L.A. to go with me, but something came up."

"Does that mean you have an extra ticket?" The kid's eyes lit up in anticipation of Jasmine's response.

"Yeah," she replied before quickly adding, "It's not for sale though," after seeing that Jackson had the same excited look in his eyes.

"You just said you had an extra one," stated Jackson, looking at Jasmine incredulously.

"I know, but—"

"Aw man, will you sell it to me? Please?" pleaded Jamal.

Jasmine looked at Jamal, a kid she had just met, but who already looked at her as though she held the key to his future. She didn't want to give him the ticket for so many reasons, the fact he was related to Jackson being one. Yet, even more important was the fact that she didn't want to be used again. Not knowing what to say, she just stood there, quiet, until Jackson spoke up.

"This should cover it," said Jackson, reaching inside his pocket to pull out a wad of cash. He handed Jasmine the money and winked.

Having offered to pay for the ticket, Jackson proved that he and his cousin weren't trying to get over on Jasmine, but she still found herself annoyed by his persistence. One mind told her to reject his offer and tell the kid, "No," but she saw the twinkle in his eye, and had heard the sincere yearning in his voice, and simply couldn't bring herself to do so.

Shoving the money inside her pocket, Jasmine looked at Jamal and said, "I don't have the ticket on me, but can give it to you tomorrow before the game." She really didn't care too much if the kid tagged along, as long as he didn't interfere with her plans to get close to Stacey.

"Cool. So, I guess it's a date," said the kid, raising and lowering his eyebrows.

"Um, no," Jackson replied before Jasmine could respond in like manner. "I'll pick you up from Auntie's and drop you off. Jasmine, I can pick you up too—"

"No thanks," she replied, cutting him off. Rolling up to the game in Jackson's ride was out of the question. Being seen with him would do nothing but spark a bunch of rumors, and the last thing she or he needed was more campus press. "Don't worry about how I'm going to get to the game. Just make sure to meet me in front of the stadium thirty minutes before it starts…and don't be late."

"He won't be," Jackson assured.

Jasmine noticed that the crowd seemed to be dispersing, and it wasn't too long before Jackson glanced down at his watch to check the time. "Looks like it's past somebody's bed time," he said, referring to his cousin, who wasn't ready to leave.

"Man, moms don't care. Why can't I hang with you tonight Jacks? Don't you have extra room at the crib?"

Jasmine didn't hear Jackson's response to his cousin because she finally caught a glimpse of Stacey off in the distance and suddenly, time stopped. She felt like she'd just been sucked inside a bubble where no other sound or sight existed except that which was emitted by Stacey. She saw him talking to a bunch of his football buddies and began to wonder how long he'd been standing there. Perhaps if she hadn't been wasting time chatting with Jackson and his cousin, she would have seen him sooner, and could have gone over to say hello.

"Look, I've gotta—" Just when Jasmine was about to ditch Jackson and his cousin, she saw Angel approach Stacey, which caused her to pause mid sentence. She heard her call out his name and watched as he turned away from his friends to greet her. Smiling widely, Stacey flashed Angel the same dimples Jasmine loved, then scooped her up in his arms. Jasmine couldn't help but stare at them, longingly, all while wishing it were she he was holding.

"Hellooo," said Jackson, waving one hand in front of Jasmine's face to get her attention.

"What?" she replied with irritation in her voice.

"I asked if you would like a ride home."

"No thanks."

"Come on. It's dark out, and I want you to be safe. I won't bite."

"I said no. Don't worry about me. I'll just catch a cab." Jasmine turned her head quickly to avoid eye contact with Jackson because she didn't want him to see the tears that were starting to well up in the corners of her eyes.

"If you say so," he replied, tugging on his cousin's jacket before directing him to follow. "Come on. I've gotta get you home."

"Aw man, that's cold Jacks."

"Remember, don't be late tomorrow!" Jasmine yelled to Jackson and his cousin as they headed out toward the street to where Jackson's car was parked.

"Oh, we won't be," Jackson shouted, as he looked back at Jasmine one last time to shoot her his devilish grin, which only caused her to regret forking over that extra ticket.

Jasmine searched the audience one last time for Stacey and Angel, but they were swept into the crowd, unable to be seen. Everyone appeared to be heading home, so she too began heading out toward the street to catch a cab ride home.

The drive home felt long, as Jasmine thought about Stacey and how she hadn't had much of an opportunity to get close to him all semester. Seeing him embrace Angel was heartwrenching, and she wished she hadn't witnessed that, for it simply reminded her of how much he was slowly slipping away from her. It was difficult for her to come to grips with the fact that she and Stacey may never be, and she struggled to fight back feelings of hopelessness. However, since the game was the following night, Jasmine knew she couldn't give up just yet, because it could end up being her lucky night. She just hoped that Stacey and the rest of the Cal Bears were victorious so that she'd have more than one reason to celebrate.

Chapter 11

It was 3:20 PM, forty minutes before game time, and Jasmine was standing outside of Memorial Stadium, waiting for Jackson and his cousin to arrive. "He'd better get here soon," she mumbled to herself before tinkering inside her purse. Her hand landed on top of her silver encrusted compact mirror, which she pulled out and flipped open. Staring at her image, Jasmine watched as her fingers twirled around the ringlets she had crafted earlier in the day. Her makeup was immaculate, and her attire was what one would call casually cute. She didn't want to overdress, because that would have made her look ridiculous. After all, this was a football game, not a party. However, she still wanted to look good for Stacey, so she put on a tight pair of low rise jeans that hugged her hips perfectly, a blue and gold Cal T-shirt, and a pair of blue and white tennis shoes. She also had the same hooded black sweater she had worn the previous night on hand, just in case it got cold later.

After putting away her compact, Jasmine found herself checking the time on her cell phone. It read 3:25 PM. Frustrated, she shoved the cell phone inside the front pocket of her jeans and watched as a mass of spectators walked past her on their way inside the stadium. "Come on

Jackson," she said to herself while placing one hand on her hip and tapping her foot against the ground.

After fiddling with the diamond heart pendant draped across her neck, Jasmine began digging inside her purse again, this time to retrieve a cigarette from the new pack she had to buy since Jackson had stolen her last one. She hadn't smoked in months, but suddenly felt the urge to light up. She reached for her lighter, and no sooner than her thumb rolled over the metal wheel to spark it, Jackson's drop-top CLK pulled up alongside the curb. The wheels on his ride came to a complete stop, and Jamal leapt out of the passenger side like a jack rabbit. "What took you so long?"

"Whaddya mean?" asked Jamal, looking down at his watch. "It's thirty minutes before game time, just like you said."

"Whatever," she replied, throwing her cigarette to the ground. The old school R&B she had faintly heard escape Jackson's car when he initially pulled up suddenly grew louder as the driver's side door swung open. With the engine still purring, Jackson stepped outside his car, looking smooth as ever. He walked around the back, then came around to the passenger side, where he leaned against the door with his legs crossed and arms folded against his chest. With loose fitting jeans, a black dress shirt, and no five o'clock shadow in sight, Jackson looked like he was about to go on a date.

"What's up, Jasmine?"

"Hello Jackson."

He stared at her for a moment, then said, "You guys have a good time, okay? And, be safe. I hear some boneheads plan to go ballistic if Cal loses."

Before Jasmine could respond, Jamal draped one arm over her shoulder, then said in an enthusiastic tone, "Oh, we will cuz!" He then turned to Jasmine and said, "Thanks again, Jasmine," before throwing his other arm around her for a hug.

Jasmine pushed the kid away and could hear Jackson laughing. "You're welcome," she said. "Just don't do that ever again, okay?"

"Okay," said the kid, as he hurried toward the entrance of the stadium.

Jackson looked at Jasmine and smiled. "Thank you, Jasmine. You really made his day."

"Don't sweat it," she said. They held each other's gaze for a moment, then Jasmine heard the kid call out her name. "I'm gonna go now."

"All right," said Jackson with a slight grin.

She turned around to catch up with the kid and handed him his ticket. After gaining approval from the attendant to enter, Jasmine immediately began heading for their seats, but Jamal stopped her.

"Hey, do you mind if I go grab some snacks first? I want to get them now so I don't miss the game."

"All right," Jasmine replied.

"You want anything?"

"No thanks. I'm gonna go sit down."

"You sure?"

"Yeah, I'm sure."

"Okay," replied the kid, scratching his temple. "Well, just so you know, Jackson asked me to take care of you, so if you need anything, just let me know, awiiight?"

The kid darted off to get his refreshments while Jasmine continued on her mission to find her seat. Once there, she remained standing and immediately began scanning the crowd for Angel. There were so many people in attendance, many of whom were wearing blue and gold—Cal's school colors, that it was impossible for Jasmine to locate her. Thus, she gave up her search and began looking down toward the field where Stanford's team was warming up. Having absolutely no interest in what was taking place, Jasmine took her seat and waited impatiently for Stacey and the rest of the Bears to enter the stadium. It felt like an eternity, but the kid finally returned with his food, and the game began. Although everyone had paid a lot of money to sit comfortably in their seats, the majority of attendees chose to stand on their feet to watch the kickoff.

The audience remained focused, as did Jasmine, on Cal's kick returner, who sprinted down the field, dodging defensive players left and right. His teammates ran in front, behind, and alongside him to act as a fluid barrier, protecting him from being pulverized by members of the opposing team. The crowd hooted and hollered, for it appeared as though he was going to make it all the way to the end zone to score the first touchdown. Yet, he ran so fast that even his teammates couldn't keep up, which left him open to being tackled by a very large guy wearing red and white, who seemed to appear out of nowhere.

Stanford's star linebacker pounced on top of Cal's kick returner, causing fans to groan as they watched the two men slide a few feet along the grass. Cardinal fans expressed a collective sigh of relief, but Cal, having advanced the ball into the red zone, kept the momentum going with subsequent plays that succeeded in scoring them the first touchdown. Spectators were ecstatic about the exciting start of the game, and many sat on the edge of their seats, anxiously awaiting another touchdown. Cal fought hard to stay on top, but Stanford definitely wasn't prepared to go out without a fight, for they scored not one, but two touchdowns by the end of the second quarter, thus placing them in the lead.

Jasmine looked to her left, then her right, and noticed a mixture of anger, disappointment, and panic start to spread across the faces of the once smiling, die-hard Cal fans. The hopelessness didn't end there, for the tension and gloom seemed to engulf the Cal team—the proof evident in the way they exited the field with heads hanging low and shoulders hunched. The team headed out of the stadium to meet with their coach, who undoubtedly scolded them during half time before strategizing their plays.

Although she wasn't too concerned about football, Jasmine wanted to see her team win. She'd watched Stacey visit the RSF on several occasions to get in shape for this very moment and therefore felt that he deserved to win. Plus, she was excited at the prospect of seeing those dimples she loved so much, cave in on his smiling face, once he'd led the team to victory. She planned to be the first to congratulate him, proving that she truly could be the great supporter and partner that he needed. Jasmine envisioned herself zooming past all the fans after the game to run onto the field where she would greet Stacey by jumping into his arms, just as she'd witnessed Angel do the night before.

As Jasmine continued to daydream about celebrating with Stacey, fans began heading toward the concession stand in droves to fuel up on junk food before the start of the third quarter. Jamal, who had been explaining plays to her since the beginning of the game, let her know that he too was about to head back down to grab more treats. Jasmine opted to remain in her seat, as she watched the uncoordinated cheerleaders perform stiff routines.

"Would you like anything?" asked Jamal.

"I'll take a hot chocolate," replied Jasmine, who noticed the drop in temperature. She put on her hooded sweater, zipping it up all the way, then sat back in her seat to continue watching the half time show.

Before darting off, Jamal looked back at Jasmine and said with a wink, "Don't go anywhere, okay." In that instance, he completely reminded her of Jackson, and she began to contemplate all the things he may have been doing while she entertained his cousin at the game. Yet, as soon as she saw the school mascot skip onto the field to help bring the cheerleaders' dumb routine to a close, her mind immediately shifted back to Stacey.

Jasmine couldn't imagine the amount of pressure Stacey must have been under to deliver a powerful performance. The game was already halfway over, and although Stanford was currently in the lead, Cal still had a chance to turn things around. For the seniors on the team, this would be their last opportunity to score a Big Game win, so she knew the pressure was extremely high for some more than others. Although she wasn't sure how the game was going to end, Jasmine knew that Stacey was a good player, and the team was lucky to have a smart guy like him for a quarterback.

Chapter 12

It was the beginning of the third quarter and the score was thirteen to seven with Stanford in the lead. Stanford was geared to receive the kick, while Cal fans hoped for a big play that would swing the game in their favor. Luckily, their prayers were answered when Cal's walk-on star buried his helmet in the chest of Stanford's kick returner, knocking the ball loose from his grip. Having successfully recovered the ball, Cal was able to begin the following play midfield.

A drop of sweat trickled down Stacey's brow as he prepared to receive the ball from his center at the line of scrimmage. He fought hard to tune out the roar of the crowd, which sounded more like muffled cries thanks to the insulation of his helmet. Steadying his mind on bringing the team's score back up, Stacey looked to his left, then his right, receiving confirmation from his offensive linemen to begin executing the play they had reviewed during half time. Nervous, yet fixed on the task at hand, Stacey took a deep breath, then called out the snap count. Moments later, he took a few steps back, then extended his arm as though he were preparing to make a pass to the tight end, but instead faked out the opposition by cradling the ball against his chest before making a mad dash toward the end zone.

Jasmine leaped to her feet to watch as Stacey sprinted down the field. He was noticeably leaner than most of his counterparts, a fact he was fully aware of and one of the many reasons a professional football career seemed an unlikely option. Knowing that his team was counting on him to successfully carry out this deceptive play, Stacey relied on his speed and agility to advance the ball toward the end zone.

Jerking his body from left to right, Stacey dodged defensive players twice his size in an ardent attempt to avoid the sting he had felt many times after getting knocked down by members of the opposing team. Taking strides like a gazelle, he watched his opponents fade into his peripheral view as he passed them by. Making it to the end zone was the only thing on his mind, and he was confident he would do so...that is, until the lights went out.

Chapter 13

Oh my gosh, oh my gosh, oh my gosh! Jasmine threw her hand across her chest as if to stop her heart from ripping through it. She was devastated after witnessing Stacey go down…and he didn't appear to be getting up. The referees and the coach huddled around him, as the audience awaited some sign, some confirmation that the quarterback would rise again. Jasmine was however on pins and needles because for her it wasn't just some injured quarterback trying to win a game that was knocked down—it was her heart that was out there on the field.

"Where are you going?"

"I've got to get down there!"

"What? Are you crazy? They're not going to let you out on the field!"

Jamal placed his hands on Jasmine's shoulders, pulling her back toward her seat. She wanted so desperately to fly down the bleachers, past all the spectators and out onto the field to make sure that Stacey was okay. Yet, Jamal was right; there was no way security would let her onto the field. Therefore, she couldn't be by Stacey's side, but also couldn't stand to sit still while he lay flat on the ground, hurt and in pain. "Okay, okay, I'm not going anywhere," she assured Jamal, who looked very concerned.

Jasmine climbed on top of her seat in an attempt to peer over the heads of those standing in front of her. She could only see the backs of the referees, the coach, and some of Stacey's teammates who were hovering over him. It felt like an eternity, but one of the referees finally turned around and waved his hands in the air. The crowd went wild, and shortly thereafter, Stacey was up on his feet. He did, however, need some assistance getting back to the sidelines.

Jasmine could tell by the way Stacey was limping that he wasn't going to make it through to the end of the game. With one arm draped around his coach's shoulder, and the other around the shoulder of the physical therapist, Stacey's head bobbed back and forth in agony. Jasmine wanted nothing more than to console him, but with Jamal ready to pounce on her if she so much as made an odd gesture toward the field, she knew it was best she sit it out like the rest of the spectators.

The game continued with Stacey on the bench and Cal still down by six points. Cal proved successful at scoring a few touchdowns after Stacey's nasty fall, but Stanford was relentless and continued to widen the gap in the score. Down nine points by the middle of the fourth quarter, you could tell Cal's players were completely agitated at this point. The fire and passion they wielded at the start of the game had waned, and it seemed they had resolved to relinquish the Big Game title to the Cardinal yet again. Looking at the opposite side of the stadium, one could see all the smiling Cardinal fans who were happy about their impending victory. Cal's side of the stadium, however, was growing more and more incensed by the minute.

Angry fans began shouting expletives towards Stanford, and the audience became more rowdy. Some spectators wearing blue and gold face paint started howling like wolves, and Jamal and Jasmine looked at each other, mutually expressing confusion in the matter. Jasmine was more concerned about Stacey's injuries than she was about the game at that point.

Time was running out in the fourth and final quarter, and it was apparent Cal had lost the game. Thus, Jamal and Jasmine decided to start heading out of the stadium, while others appeared to be bent on waiting for the clock to run out before declaring a winner. Jasmine didn't want to get caught up in the mad dash to make it back out to the street, so she grabbed her purse and made sure Jamal was behind her before walking down the stairs of the stadium.

Jamal and Jasmine made it to ground level the moment the game ended. Thirty to twenty-one was the final score. Although many had decided to stay in the stands until the last minute, others had the same idea as Jamal and Jasmine, so the two of them found themselves gridlocked, as they attempted to make their way toward the exit. Jasmine felt pressure in her back and sides as spectators anxiously fought their way toward the exit. Those in the rear continued pressing forward, ultimately pushing Jasmine into the back of a male spectator, who seemed to have the funk of sweat, beer, and nachos emanating from his pores. She was forced to cover her nose with her hand in order to block the smell, then glanced back at Jamal, who had once been right behind her, but was now mashed in between two other people a few feet behind. He nodded to show that he could still see her, so she resumed her push forward to advance another half inch with the rest of the crowd.

Jasmine was still worried about Stacey, but at the rate they were moving, she'd never make it to him in time to see how he was doing. He and the rest of the team were probably in the locker room by now. Besides, she was starting to feel icky, thanks to all the musty bodies that were pressed up against her, and wanted nothing more than to break free from the crowd. Yet, just when she thought the situation couldn't get any worse, loud screams began pouring in from the same direction of the field. The next thing she knew, people in front of her started running like crazy, and the path that was once blocked suddenly became clear, as if floodgates had been opened. Before she could get her feet to follow suit, Jasmine felt herself being propelled forward, as frantic spectators rushed her from behind. She had to run or else she'd be trampled by the stampede that had suddenly formed.

When Jasmine found herself in the clear, she took a moment to look back for Jamal, but he was nowhere in sight. About half a second later, she found herself forced to run again, as two heavyset women with fear in their eyes charged full speed in her direction. Attempting to lunge forward with no success, Jasmine looked down and found that her sweater was snagged on one of the rails leading up the stairs of the stadium. With the two women still heading in her direction, threatening to knock her down, she frantically unzipped the sweater and wriggled her way out of it. As soon as she had been set free, Jasmine took off running in the same direction as the people in front of her. She had absolutely no idea what was going on, but knew that she had to get the heck out of dodge, quick.

Chapter 14

Several cars whizzed past the stadium, making it extremely difficult for Jackson to find a parking space. Had he known the streets would be so congested, he would have tried to make it back sooner. He assumed most of the spectators would be getting home by way of mass transit, and therefore wasn't prepared for the battle he faced with other drivers, who were also trying to provide curbside service to those leaving the game. As he circled the block in anticipation of snagging a spot the moment it became vacant, Jackson took note of the demeanor of those exiting the stadium.

Having not tuned in to the game on the radio or television, Jackson was unaware of the final outcome. Yet, the gleeful expressions he noticed plastered across the faces of fans wearing Stanford's team colors made their team's victory evident. At first glance, nothing seemed amiss, as spectators appeared to be exiting the stadium in a calm and rational manner. Jackson did however observe a few scowls on the faces of Cal fans, but simply chalked them up to evidence of a bitter loss. It wasn't until he caught distressed looks on some people's faces and saw that they were no longer walking, but running toward the street in droves, that he realized something was terribly wrong.

The riot, the very thing Jackson had warned Jasmine and Jamal about was taking place, causing folks to panic, and sheer pandemonium to ensue. Determined to save his cousin and the object of his desire from the melee, Jackson swerved his Mercedes CLK over to the right, completely disregarding his own safety, and the safety of those in the car he dangerously cut off before securing an illegal parking spot in the red zone. He then made a mad dash toward the stadium.

Security was busy battling the source of the commotion, which Jackson soon learned was taking place out on the field, so there was no one to stop him from entering the stadium. He immediately found himself having to fight his way past the sea of spectators, many of whom were headed in the opposite direction. However, adrenaline seemed to be pumping through his veins, providing enough strength and endurance to carry out his mission.

"Jamal! Jasmine!" Jackson desperately called out to the two people he hoped to find unscathed by the disorderly flock of rabble rousers, but received no response to calm his nerves. Instead, he became further distraught once he finally made it to the stands and found a familiar looking sweater hanging from one of the railings.

"Jackson!"

Just as Jackson reached for the sweater that closely resembled the one he saw Jasmine wear the night before, he heard someone shout his name. Stunned, he turned his head to the left and spied Jamal running towards him with his shirt in tatters. "Are you okay?"

"Yeah…I'm cool," replied Jamal, who was gasping for air.

"Where's Jasmine?"

"What?"

"Jasmine!"

"I—uh—I dunno. I lost her a long time ago."

Furious, Jackson grabbed Jamal by what was left of his collar, and practically lifted his scrawny body off the ground. "What do you mean you lost her? I told you to look after her!"

"I know, but I got pushed, and she, she—"

Before Jamal could finish his sentence, Jackson released his grip, allowing him to regain his footing. Handing his keys to Jamal, he instructed: "Go outside to the curb and wait in the car. If the cops come, I want you to circle the block until Jasmine and I come out."

"But I only have my permit!"

"Just do as I say!"

"Okay," replied Jamal, jittery and confused.

Trusting that Jamal would make it out to the street okay, Jackson sprinted off in the direction of the field to look for Jasmine. He was scared to think of what condition she might be in considering that Jamal, who was supposed to be her bodyguard, was banged up and bruised. Observing a mass of people who were fighting, yelling, and tearing things apart out on the field only added to his frustration. To make matters worse, Jackson spotted two young men dressed in blue and gold, dangerously climbing the goal post at the far end of the field. With jaws agape and faces contorted, the two bold climbers appeared to be shouting something to the crowd below, but there was no way for Jackson to distinguish what they were saying over the din of the crowd below. Although he began to feel a bit overwhelmed by all the confusion, he refused to allow his efforts to be thwarted by it.

Shoving and pushing rambunctious young men out of his way, Jackson resembled a football player as he headed down the field toward the goal post. Cal may have possibly won the game had some of its players possessed the same drive and passion he was now exhibiting. Although it wasn't his intent to add to the ruckus, Jackson was willing to do whatever it took to rescue the woman he had been dying to capture for months.

Chapter 15

Jasmine should have followed her instincts and turned left instead of heading in the same direction as those in front of her, for she thought they were leading her away from all the chaos. Yet, once she made it out onto the field, she realized they had landed her smack dab in the middle of it all. Perhaps if she hadn't been trying to escape the two women behind her, she would have had a moment to orient herself and move quickly toward the exit. However, she now had no clue as to how she was ever going to make it out of the stadium.

Fans upset over Cal's loss made their anger known. Some went as far as fighting with Stanford spectators, while others stood around and jeered. It was getting dark, and there was so much madness taking place that Jasmine could barely see straight. She looked toward the end zone, hoping the far end of the field would provide some sort of refuge, but was horrified upon witnessing two young men, who looked drunk and out of sorts, dangerously climbing the goal post. Feeling helpless, Jasmine stood paralyzed, afraid of making what could turn out to be another wrong move.

Just when she thought things couldn't get any worse, her ears perked up as a woman standing close by shrieked loudly while pointing toward the goal post. The two young men had succeeded at reaching the top of the structure and were now clinging on for dear life, as the posts swayed back and forth. Those who were once fighting stopped to watch the terrifying scene, for it was clear they were doomed to fall at any second.

Jasmine was afraid to stay where she was, but couldn't seem to figure a way out of the mess. The fear was so crippling that she could feel anxiety rage throughout her body. Breathing heavily, Jasmine grasped her chest and began spacing out. Almost instantly, her eyesight grew dim and her knees turned weak. The only thing that kept her from collapsing was the sight of Jackson, who broke through the wall of people to come to her rescue.

Chapter 16

Jasmine spotted Jackson and let out a huge sigh of relief. His presence settled her nerves, allowing her to regain her composure. Peering into his eyes as he approached, Jasmine realized that this was the first time she found comfort in those dark, mysterious orbs. Without reservation, she melted against his body, her arms draped over his shoulders. The gesture was dramatic, but it conveyed her gratitude in a way that words could not describe. Jackson immediately responded in kind by enveloping her in his arms. They remained in each other's embrace for a while, showing no concern for the disorder taking place around them.

"Let's get out of here," Jackson said finally, throwing them back into the moment.

"Okay," Jasmine replied.

Grabbing Jasmine's hand, Jackson led the way as the two of them attempted to escape the riot. Thanks to his height and build, they were able to push past people in a way that Jasmine couldn't on her own. Suddenly, she knew what it felt like to be rescued by a knight in shining armor. Jasmine didn't want to fall victim to another man's charm and strength, yet even she had to admit that allowing Jackson to rescue her gave her a surge of energy she'd never experienced before. Interlocking her slender fingers with his, she attempted to remain close, unwilling to risk losing him or that warm feeling of security.

They eventually made their way out of the stadium and to Jackson's car, which was occupied by Jamal, who looked nervous and beat down. "I'm so glad y'all made it! Get in!" he yelled, before squeezing into the backseat so that Jackson could take over. Jackson opened the passenger side door and made sure Jasmine was safe before entering.

"Buckle up," he said before pulling off.

"Man, that was craaa-zy!" stated Jamal. "I thought we'd never get out of there!"

Silent, Jasmine looked over at Jackson, who stared back at her. She felt awkward, as if she were suddenly looking at a different person.

"I'm going to take you home first, okay?" said Jackson, looking at Jamal through the rear-view mirror.

Jackson turned on the radio, and the three of them remained silent as they headed to Jamal's house in Richmond, a city adjacent to Berkeley. All it took was a few minutes on the always heavily trafficked highway I-80, and they were there. Jackson left Jasmine alone in the car as he stepped out to see his cousin to the door. They said their goodbyes, then Jackson headed back to the car to take Jasmine home. Shifting uncomfortably in her seat, Jasmine began to feel uneasy about the whole situation. She and Jackson hadn't said anything to each other since they left the stadium, and she still couldn't believe how happy she had been to see him out on the field…or that she had hugged him.

"Hey, you okay?" asked Jackson, placing one hand on her shoulder. He sensed her discomfort, as she sat quietly in the passenger seat, stiff.

"Yeah…I'm fine."

"I know things have been a little crazy, but I'm going to take you home and everything's going to be all right, okay?" Jackson tried to offer some encouraging words, then moved his hand up to Jasmine's face, as he softly brushed her cheek. Her discomfort intensified, and she found herself becoming agitated. She hoped he didn't think that simply because he had saved her from a bad situation that meant she was going to melt in his hands like butter.

"Actually, you can just drop me off on the corner of Shattuck and Durant. I can walk home from there," she said, trying to sound tough.

"Sure," replied Jackson, although the expression on his face and the sarcasm in his voice stated otherwise. Sure enough, once they made it back to Berkeley, Jackson insisted on taking Jasmine home.

"There's no way I'm letting you walk around here alone, in the dark. There could still be some crazy Cal fans out and about for all you know." Always persistent, Jackson wasn't going to let Jasmine call the shots. "Now, are we going to drive around in circles all night, or are you going to tell me how to get to your place?" Before she could respond, Jackson paused, then looked at Jasmine with the devilish grin she'd grown accustomed to seeing. "Or," he continued, "You could just spend the night at my place."

"Right," she replied, her voice laced with the same sarcasm he had spoken with earlier. "Turn left up here," she said, pointing to the street in front of them. Jasmine knew she was crazy for letting Jackson see where she lived, but figured she'd be even crazier for allowing him to take her back to his place for the night. "That's my place coming up on the right," she said once they finally made it onto her street. After pulling up behind one of the cars parked on her block, Jackson shut off the engine and prepared to exit.

"What are you doing?"

"Walking you to the door."

"That's not necessary."

Jackson rolled his eyes and stepped out of the car. Jasmine also stepped out and to her surprise, found Jackson standing in front of her the moment she planted her foot onto the curb. She tried to turn around to close the door, but he stood so close that he practically had her pinned up against the car. Without breaking eye contact, Jackson reached around Jasmine and shut her door.

"Thanks for the ri—"

Jasmine's words were interrupted by Jackson, who firmly pressed his lips against hers. He kissed her once, then pulled back to gauge her reaction. Stunned, Jasmine stared at him, and he grabbed her again, this time kissing her longer. She had to be honest and admit that she actually enjoyed the kiss, for she fully participated and even rested one hand against the back of his neck.

After a few moments of lip locking, Jackson pulled away and said, "Let's go inside."

"Um, I don't think so," Jasmine replied, putting an end to his advances. True, he had helped her, and yes, she was grateful, but not *that* grateful! "If you think I'm going to sleep with you because you've helped me tonight, you're wrong!" she stated firmly, pulling further away from him. Jasmine threw her purse over her shoulder and pushed past Jackson as she headed toward the front door of her apartment. Yet, she was only able to take a few steps forward when Jackson suddenly grabbed her by the arm, spinning her back around.

"Wait. What makes you think I want to sleep with you?"

"Are you kidding?" she asked, looking at him incredulously.

"Look, you're fine and all, but you're not *that* fine."

With that, Jasmine snatched her arm from Jackson and turned back around to continue heading toward the door. However, this time he jumped in front of her.

"Wait. That's not what I meant. What I meant to say is what makes you think every man that crosses your path just wants to sleep with you?"

"I never said *every* man. I was simply referring to you. Besides, what am I supposed to think with all the sexual innuendos you throw around?"

"Look, Jasmine, I know I flirt with you a lot, but I really just want to get to know you better, that's all. I'm not who…or what you think I am. Just give me a chance and you'll see."

Jasmine wasn't sure what it was exactly, but there was something about Jackson in that moment that made her believe him. Perhaps it had something to do with the fact that his eyes, which once seemed so intense, now appeared soft, as though they were pleading with her to give him a chance. All she saw was sincerity, and found herself getting lost in the promise they held.

"Okay," she said, finally relenting. "Where do we go from here?"

"Well, we can start by having dinner. How about Friday night?"

"Friday will work."

"Cool. I'll pick you up around eight."

"Okay."

Jackson waited until Jasmine made it inside her apartment before heading back to his car. She was actually really glad that he had taken her home because she wouldn't have felt safe if he hadn't. She wasn't sure what was happening between she and Jackson, the same man she had vowed to stay away from, but was somewhat intrigued by the whole situation—so much so that she went to bed pondering the possibility of their union, not once giving a single thought to what happened at the game, or Stacey.

Chapter 17

The week following the Big Game was a blur. Jasmine was so busy doing last minute studying for winter finals that she didn't have much time to think about Stacey or Jackson for that matter. When Friday finally rolled around however, all she could think about was Jackson, and their date that night.

Normally Jasmine didn't stress over dates, because she felt like she was in the driver's seat. Most guys were so happy to take her out that they would go out of their way to impress her, making the night a nerve-wracking event for them. A lot of them behaved clumsily or ended up tongue tied because of their nervousness, forcing Jasmine to be the chill one, which she loved because it enabled her to maintain a level head and not be swept off her feet by their actions. Going out with Jackson was different though, because he wasn't your run-of-the-mill college boy.

A typical date with the average eighteen or nineteen-year-old male usually involves a trip to the local movie theater. You might get dinner if you're lucky, and probably not a good one at that. Thus, the fact that Jackson was taking Jasmine to Chez Panisse for dinner, one of the most expensive and highly rated French restaurants in town was no minor detail.

Jasmine felt knots form in her stomach as she searched her closet for an outfit to wear. Although she had a ton of options to choose from, she found herself at a complete loss, because she wanted to make sure that she wore something that suited the caliber of the restaurant, but wasn't too flashy or sexy, causing Jackson to get any bright ideas. After a few drags on a cigarette and several minutes of deliberating, she finally decided on a simple black dress with spaghetti straps. It was sophisticated enough for the locale, but not so dressy that it would give Jackson the wrong impression. She didn't want him to think she was taking the whole date thing too seriously. She still couldn't believe she had agreed to go out with him.

Jasmine sat at her vanity and began perfecting her spiral curls with a curling iron when she heard a knock at the door. Jumping up from the table, she checked herself in the mirror one last time before sliding her feet inside the three-inch silver stilettos she'd decided to wear. She then rushed over to the door and reached for the knob, but decided not to open it just yet. Remembering the cigarette she had smoked earlier, Jasmine grabbed a can of air freshener from the bathroom and sprayed three mists of fragrance in the air before returning to the door.

"Hi," she said to Jackson, who stood at her door, looking exceptionally handsome in his black slacks, cream-colored button down shirt and black blazer. With his goatee trimmed to perfection and skin looking like creamy chocolate mousse, Jackson looked like he had just stepped off the cover of GQ magazine. Jasmine tried to appear unmoved by his appearance, but found herself having to take a deep breath in order to maintain her composure. It became even harder for her to gather herself once she caught a whiff of his cologne, for the scent caused her knees to go weak.

"You look beautiful, as always," stated Jackson, looking deep into Jasmine's eyes. He moved one arm forward to present her with a fresh bouquet of roses. She tried her best to appear unimpressed.

"Thanks," she said before taking hold of the bouquet. She then headed toward the kitchen to find a vase to place the flowers in while Jackson followed.

"Nice little place you've got here."

Jasmine reached inside the cabinet to retrieve a vase and noticed that her hands were trembling as she grabbed hold of one she felt best suited the large arrangement of long stemmed roses. She hated feeling nervous and was unsure as to how she was going to make it through the night without giving Jackson the satisfaction of seeing her sweat. That was until he said something that reminded her that it was still Jackson Taylor, the man with the tendency to annoy her, who she was about to spend the evening with.

"Yep, this place is nice," Jackson reiterated as he surveyed the area. "Although, I could do without the faint scent of cigarette butts, masked behind a hint of vanilla."

"I know you love Virginia Slims since you stole my last pack, so I thought I'd light up in your honor," Jasmine replied, shooting him an equally sarcastic remark. It helped add levity to the situation, for her hands ceased trembling.

"Aw, thanks honey," said Jackson, responding in kind.

After placing the flowers inside a vase, Jasmine turned around to face her date. "You ready?"

"After you," he replied, gesturing as an usher would when directing one to a seat.

The two of them headed outside to where Jackson's car was parked, and like a true gentleman, he opened the passenger door and helped her inside. The ride to the restaurant was a short one, which Jasmine was glad about because it meant that she didn't have to talk to him for very long.

"We're here," Jackson announced before turning off the engine.

Jasmine reached for the knob to open her door, but Jackson stopped her. "Wait. I'll get that." He stepped outside the car and walked around to the passenger side, then offered his hand to her, but she pretended as though she didn't see it and proceeded toward the entrance of the restaurant. Once inside, they were seated immediately, for Jackson had made reservations in advance. The waiter led them to a secluded spot near the back of the restaurant where the lighting was dim, and a bottle of champagne sat on top of the table.

"Mademoiselle," said Jackson while pulling out Jasmine's chair.

They sat down, and Jackson stared at Jasmine from the opposite end of the table. She got the impression that he was searching her face for a reaction to their evening thus far, but she simply averted her eyes from his and cracked open the menu. "So, what's good here?" she asked, pretending to be deeply engrossed in the various dining options.

"Well, their menu changes daily, but I can assure you that everything they serve here is good. Have you ever tried escargot?"

"No, and I don't plan to."

"Why not?" asked Jackson with a wide grin. "You only live once."

"No thanks. I think I'll just try the chicken and play it safe." The waiter returned to the table and Jackson let him know that they were ready to order.

"Qu'est-ce que vous voudriez mademoiselle?" The waiter spoke to Jasmine in French, and she had absolutely no idea what he said, but could tell by the inflection in his voice that he had asked her a question. She looked at Jackson, expecting him to mimic her puzzled expression, but he instead replied to the waiter, and nearly knocked her out of her chair.

"Elle aura le poulet avec des pommes de terre et une petite salade."

"Et pour vous?"

"Je vais avoir la poisson avec des haricots verts."

"Merci," said the waiter, as he collected their menus.

"Where did you learn that?" asked Jasmine once the waiter had stepped away. She tried to sound more inquisitive than excited.

"Oh, it's just a little something I picked up during my summers in France." Jackson could tell Jasmine was impressed, so he flashed her his signature, devilish grin.

"You've been to France?"

"Yep. You'd love it, especially Paris. Who knows, maybe the two of us can go one day."

Jasmine ignored Jackson's remark and asked, "When did you last go?"

"Um, about two years ago. I took some time off after undergrad to explore, you know, enjoy life a little. My family and I used to vacation there all the time when I was a kid. My brother and I finally decided to go by ourselves for once—we had an unbelievable time. We spent a week in France, then flew to Spain where we stayed another week."

"You have a brother?"

"Yeah—two to be exact. Xavier is a lot older than I—he's in his forties. He's my father's son from a previous marriage. The other, Caleb, is twenty-two and just graduated from Harvard. That's where I did my undergrad."

"You did your undergrad at Harvard?" At this point, Jasmine was in complete awe of Jackson, so there was no hiding her enthusiasm.

"Mhmm," he replied through pursed lips. "My father wanted us to attend his alma mater, NYU, but the two of us chose Harvard instead. It's such a shame how much we've disappointed him." Jackson shook his head sarcastically, and Jasmine couldn't help but let out a soft giggle. He then stared at her and smiled, causing her to feel a bit uneasy. She shifted uncomfortably in her seat, but Jackson gave her no respite, as he kept his eyes steady on her face. Not wanting him to think she'd allowed him to intimidate her, Jasmine decided to take the reigns for a minute.

"Now that I know some things about Mr. Taylor that I never knew before, how 'bout we dispel some of the myths," she said, leaning against the table.

"What myths?"

"You know, the rumors that have been floating around campus about you."

"I wasn't aware there were any," replied Jackson with a smirk.

"Well, there are," affirmed Jasmine, looking dead in his eyes.

"Okay then, shoot. Ask me anything."

"Well, let's start with your age. Some say you're thirty."

"Do I look thirty?"

"I dunno," she quickly replied. Jasmine didn't want Jackson to think she had contemplated his age, or anything else about him for that matter.

"Actually, I'm twenty-six," said Jackson, who could sense Jasmine's relief. She had just turned twenty and was a bit happy to discover that he wasn't that much older than she, for it made him seem a little less threatening. "I graduated from Harvard at twenty-one," he continued. "I took some time off to explore my options, then decided to go back to school for my master's in business."

"Why Cal?"

"Why Cal? I didn't think a Cal student would ever ask me that."

"I know Haas is one of the best schools in the nation for business, but—"

"But what? That says it all."

"I mean, you came from Harvard though. Why the big leap to California?"

"For one, my family is in Vegas now, so this places me closer to home. Plus, I've done the Ivy League thing and was looking for a different experience. Cal is a great public university and it's very affordable."

"Affordable? Like money is an issue for you."

"Excuse me?"

"Come on," said Jasmine, looking at Jackson with skepticism. "The way you dress, the car you drive—it's clear you're not lacking funds. Word on the street is that your family owns a casino in—"

Before she could finish her sentence, Jackson threw his head back and belted out a laugh so loud that Jasmine looked around the restaurant to see if any of the patrons were disturbed by it.

"I'm sorry," he said, trying to regain his composure. "I guess there really are myths floating around campus about me. It makes me feel like a legend."

"Yeah, I guess," she replied before taking a sip of water. "I asked some girl in my lit class about you and—"

"So, you asked about me, huh?"

Feeling totally caught off guard, Jasmine looked at Jackson and started stuttering. "I—uh—I, I meant to say—"

"That's cool," he said, cutting her off. He stared at her with those dark eyes of his and grinned like a child who had just unwrapped a Christmas gift to find that Santa had given him exactly what he wanted. Jasmine felt like jumping up from the table and leaving, but the waiter returned with their food, diffusing some of the tension that had built up between them.

Jackson was right; the food was delicious, and Jasmine took small bites to ensure that she didn't look like a pig in front of him. She thought they were going to finish the meal in silence, but then Jackson spoke, "You know, things aren't always as they appear, Jasmine. True, my family is very well off, but we've worked hard to get to where we are today. My father's in real estate and has been fortunate enough to sell homes to the rich and famous. He's spent his life making sure that my brothers and I understand how to work smart, not hard, so that we can still enjoy life. He's one of the main reasons why I've decided to pursue my MBA. I already have my real estate license, but I figure that truly understanding business will only help me further along in my career."

"That's cool," said Jasmine in between bites.

"People make assumptions based on perception, but you don't really know someone until you take the time to interact with them," stated Jackson. "Anyway, enough about me," he continued. "I want to learn more about you Miss, Miss…" Jackson paused for a moment, then asked, "What is your last name by the way?"

"Fairchild."

"Fairchild? Hmm, I've never heard of that before. Sounds so regal." Jackson stared off into space, then said, "Anyway, back to what I was saying—"

"What rumors have you heard about me, aside from the usual?" asked Jasmine, interrupting his speech.

"What is the usual?"

"That I'm a cold, heartless man-eater—and that's putting it lightly."

"Hmm, I didn't hear that one," said Jackson, smiling.

"Sure," she replied, also smiling.

"I'm sure plenty of things have been said about you and me that don't necessarily place us in the best light," he assured. "But, that's cool with me because I don't like to prejudge or misjudge people based on hearsay."

"That's good to know," said Jasmine before taking another bite of food. She wanted to prod Jackson more, but was a little afraid of what the outcome might be. Yet, she figured she had nothing to lose, so she asked, "What have you heard about me that you choose not to believe?"

Jackson took a bite of his food and stared down at his plate for a moment. He then wiped his mouth with his napkin before lifting his head. "Well, I normally don't like to talk about things like this, especially on a first date, but…" he paused to contemplate his next statement, then continued, "Hey, it's not really important, is it?"

"I want to know," said Jasmine, her curiosity intensified.

Jackson took a sip of his water, then returned the glass to the table. "All right, but I think it'll cause more harm than good. Just know that I didn't want to go there."

Jasmine gave Jackson a look that conveyed her lack of concern for his feelings in the matter. She hadn't changed her mind—she wanted to know.

"Well, to put it nicely, the rumor is that you have quite an elaborate list of previous male suitors."

"And of course for a woman, that means that I'm promiscuous, right?" Jasmine looked Jackson dead in his eyes as she awaited his response. If that was the worst thing people were saying about her, then nothing had changed. That rumor had been following her around since high school. "You know," she began, while looking down at her ravaged plate, "It's funny how a man gets applauded for the number of women he sleeps with, and a woman gets condemned."

"So…it's true?" asked Jackson with apprehension in his voice.

"No!" Jasmine snapped. "True, I've dated plenty of guys, but I didn't have sex with all of them. Not that it's any of your business, but I've actually only been with one person, yet I'm sure nobody would believe that."

Jackson sat back in his chair and eyeballed Jasmine as though what she'd said was truly a revelation. Jasmine leaned forward in her chair, placing her forearms on the table. "It's like you said earlier, you may find that a lot of what you thought to be true about a person really isn't."

"I'm sorry if I came off—"

"That's okay. I'm used to it. Besides, according to my sources, you don't have the best track record either."

Jackson adjusted his shirt collar and sat up straight. "Unfortunately for me, some of it's true," he said, looking a little sheepish. That wasn't an expression Jasmine thought she'd ever see on a man like Jackson Taylor. He was so self-assured that she figured he'd wear the notches on his belt with pride like most men. Yet, he was showing her little by little that he wasn't the man she'd initially perceived him to be.

"It's not something I'm proud of," he continued, "But it happens. I guess you can say that I sowed my wild oats and am now ready for a new chapter in my life."

"That's funny, 'cause I know a lot of men who would be more than willing to chase tail well into their thirties, forties even," said Jasmine, gazing at him in disbelief.

"Yeah, well, I figure if you want something different, then you have to do something different. That type of lifestyle doesn't offer many challenges, and I need a woman who can keep me on my toes." Jackson held Jasmine's gaze, and she could tell by the look in his eyes that she was the woman to whom he was referring. She wanted to change the subject, but before he or she could say anything, the waiter reappeared and asked if they wanted dessert.

Given the meager portions offered by most French restaurants, Jasmine could have definitely gone for some dessert, but her gut told her to decline so that she and Jackson could move closer to the end of their date. Jackson however had no intention of seeing her off early, so he ordered some sorbet for himself, while she tried her best to conceal her rattled nerves.

"Sorbet? I'm surprised you didn't order a cupcake," Jasmine said sarcastically.

Smiling, Jackson replied, "Unfortunately, they don't serve those here, but believe me, if they did, I'd order one." Jackson paused for a moment as he looked into Jasmine's eyes, then said, "You know, now that I think about it, you sort of remind me of a cupcake."

"Oh Lord," said Jasmine, rolling her eyes. "Let me guess, because I'm sweet. Come on, how cheesy can you be?"

"I wasn't going to say that," Jackson replied, looking serious. "You remind me of a cupcake because when I was a kid, my mother would buy me one whenever I was feeling down. When I fell off the monkey bars in elementary school and broke my arm, she showed up in the nurse's office with a vanilla cupcake with cream cheese frosting. When my pet lizard died, she bought me a chocolate cupcake with vanilla frosting, and when I lost my first track meet in high school, she bought me a vanilla cupcake with strawberry frosting and sprinkles. No matter how down I was feeling, those cupcakes always seemed to do the trick. They tasted so good that for a moment, I forgot about everything that was bothering me. They never failed to lift my spirits, and soon had me smiling again."

"So what the heck does that have to do with me?"

"Because the first day I saw you on campus, I had just left my professor's office to discuss a bad grade he had given me on one of my take-home assignments. I tried to debate my way up to a higher mark, but he wouldn't budge. I was pissed beyond belief, but a few minutes later, I spotted you and suddenly, I wasn't upset anymore."

Jasmine was at a loss for words, so she just looked at Jackson and didn't say anything. His explanation may have sounded like a cheap line to the ears of a passerby, but his delivery and expression said otherwise.

Once Jackson had his fill of raspberry sorbet, he picked up the tab, then he and Jasmine headed down to the Berkeley Marina for a "romantic" evening stroll. They ended up spending the rest of the evening walking up and down the pier, which was barely tolerable given that it was cold out. The light wrap Jasmine had brought along to cover up with wasn't enough to stave off the tiny goose bumps that were starting to form along her upper arms. Jackson took notice and wrapped his blazer around her shoulders. The warmth from his body, mixed in with the pleasant scent of his cologne made Jasmine want to keep it on for hours. She held onto both sides of the coat so that it wouldn't slip off, and began to imagine that it was Stacey's coat draped around her.

During their stroll, Jackson and Jasmine talked about the craziness of the Big Game, their likes and dislikes about school, and the eerie color and brightness of the full moon that was out. About an hour later, they began to feel the air grow colder, and finally decided to call it a night. When they arrived back at Jasmine's place, Jackson walked her to her door and she offered him a kiss on the cheek, but he grabbed her by the waist and planted a passionate kiss on her lips. Jasmine tried hard to ignore the tingling sensation in her toes as she stepped inside her apartment and wished Jackson a good night.

Jasmine had to admit that Jackson shattered every expectation she had of him being a self-centered jerk, and actually showed genuine interest in her on their date. He was polite, courteous, and actually fun to be around, and despite the stony expressions she had displayed throughout the evening, she was extremely impressed by his candor and level of sophistication. Jasmine was also amazed by Jackson's knowledge of French, although she would never tell him that. She had to play it cool and keep in mind that Stacey was still number one in her heart…although, Jackson was running a really close second.

Chapter 18

Jackson and Jasmine started hanging out frequently after their first date. Jasmine went home to spend time with her father during the winter break, and when she returned to her apartment in January, there were a dozen, long-stemmed roses waiting for her on her doorstep. She also had an email for every day she was gone waiting for her in the inbox of her school email account.

In his emails, Jackson expressed how much he missed Jasmine, and was glad that she had finally given him a chance to take her out. He said he wanted to have many more dates like the first one and that hopefully their time together would only get better. Jasmine was shocked yet intrigued by his gesture, and wondered if she were allowing herself to get caught in a trap so deep, it would be extremely difficult to get out.

Jasmine actually thought a lot about Jackson during the break and was scared to admit how much she'd fallen for him. She still however had visions of Stacey in the back of her mind, because as far as she was concerned, that was still an avenue yet to be explored. Angel was probably nursing his wounds and helping him prepare for the spring, but Jasmine was prepared to deal with her if necessary. Although she still was unsure of how she was ever going to get Stacey to look at her and only her, she considered that challenge to be less risky than pursuing a relationship with Jackson.

Stacey and Jasmine had different majors, so they didn't have any classes together that semester. She therefore rarely saw him on campus and occasionally caught him working out at the RSF, but that didn't provide her with much opportunity to talk to him. He was seriously working with a personal trainer to strengthen his leg after the break he suffered during the Big Game. Although Jasmine made sure to tell him how sorry she was about his injury, she had decided to back off of him for the most part because she wanted to be respectful of his recovery and avoid coming off too strong.

In the meantime, Jasmine and Jackson were developing a friendship that oddly enough, seemed to be growing into something more serious than Jasmine had ever intended for it to be. It began slowly, as they started hanging out at cafés between classes, then progressed to the point where they were talking on the phone constantly and having dates every Friday and Saturday night. Jasmine really didn't know what to make of her relationship with Jackson, but one thing was certain; he had become such a huge part of her life that she had no choice but to tell Missy about him.

Hearing any name other than Stacey's was like breathing a breath of fresh air for Missy, because as far as she was concerned, Jasmine was living in a fantasy world when it came to her true object of desire. The fact that Jackson was actually "courting" her, as Missy put it, was worth more than her seemingly frivolous encounters with Stacey. After hearing about their first date, the emails and flowers he sent, and the way he made sure she walked on the inside and not the outer part of the sidewalk when they walked down the street, Jackson became the prototype for Mr. Right in Missy's eyes. The only thing left was for Jasmine to introduce her to him, and she wanted to do so, quick, before she started to think that he too was a figment of her imagination.

"Missy, this is Jackson Taylor. Jackson, this is Missy Mae Holden."

"Nice to finally meet you young man," said Missy with a grin. "I've heard so much about you."

"Oh you have, have you," replied Jackson before quickly shooting Jasmine a satisfied grin. "Hopefully it's been nothing but good things," he added before lightly kissing the back of Missy's wrinkled hand.

"It certainly has," assured Missy, looking at Jackson and smiling. "Stand back and let me get a good look at you." Missy reached for her glasses on the nightstand next to her bed. She put them on and studied Jackson carefully from head to toe, as if the materialization of the man Jasmine had spoken about was too good to be true. "You're a fine young man, indeed," she said, further expressing her approval of him. "You don't happen to have a single grandfather, do you?"

"Missy!" yelled Jasmine before the three of them erupted with laughter.

"No...I don't," Jackson eventually replied, still fighting off laughter. "Unfortunately, I never got to meet any of my grandparents, but if they'd lived long enough to be in my life, I hope they'd be as colorful as you."

Missy was definitely a character, and seeing her interact with Jackson made Jasmine appreciate her even more. Jackson had so much fun talking to her that he wondered why Jasmine hadn't introduced him to her sooner.

"I wish I were young and spry like y'all two again," said Missy, looking wistfully at the young pair. "I've gotten so old that I can barely laugh without my back hurting."

"Here, let me get that for you," said Jasmine, raising Missy's pillow so that she could sit up more comfortably in her bed. Jasmine helped Missy ease her body back up against the pillow, while Jackson took a seat in a chair nearby and watched. Feeling more at ease, Missy continued to entertain Jackson and Jasmine with numerous stories about her life, which caused them to laugh at certain parts, and be somber at others. Then, after a few hours had passed, Jackson and Jasmine prepared to depart.

"It was so wonderful meeting you young man," stated Missy. "You take care of yourself, you hear?"

"I will ma'am. It was nice meeting you too."

"Oh, and please take care of my Jazz for me, will you? She needs someone to reel her in at times."

"Missy!"

"I dunno," replied Jackson, completely ignoring Jasmine's attempt at scolding Missy for her outrageous insinuation. "She's kinda hard to tame, but I'll do my best." He and Missy continued to talk about her as though she weren't in the room.

"Please do," said Missy. "Oh, and if you don't mind, I'd like to talk to Jasmine alone for a moment."

"No problem," Jackson replied before heading toward the door. He told Jasmine that he would wait for her out in the hall.

Jasmine approached Missy to see what she wanted, and as soon as she made it to her bedside, Missy grabbed her by the hand and drew her in close. "Now *that* is a man," she said, looking at Jasmine intently. "I can tell by the way he looks at you that he really cares for you."

"Oh Missy—"

"Just listen to me for a second." Jasmine tried to stop Missy from talking to her about Jackson, because she knew it wasn't going to do anything but make her think about him more seriously, something she was trying so desperately to avoid. Yet, Missy interrupted her and insisted on saying her piece. "I've had my share of ups and downs when it comes to relationships," she continued, "So I know what love is and what it isn't. That man out there loves you and you need to take him seriously. I know how you can be sometimes, but trust me when I say that you have a good thing there."

Missy paused for a moment and removed her glasses. She then looked Jasmine in her eyes and squinted as though she were trying to look inside her to see if what she said had actually registered. Jasmine looked away for a moment, because Missy's stare was so intense, it was almost too much for her to bear. However, she soon turned her eyes back on Missy's to let her know that she was listening. "Whatever you do," she continued, "Don't mess this up because of fear. Love is a risk worth taking, and believe me when I say that good men—no, good people don't come around often, so you better appreciate what you have before it's gone."

Jasmine heard everything Missy said, but wasn't quite ready to digest it all. She was right in that love was a risk, which is exactly what Jasmine feared. Not knowing if Jackson's charm and sentiments towards her were sincere was like taking a gamble on the unknown, when she felt her best bet would be to play it safe and stick with Stacey, who she felt more comfortable with. True, many women would have been thrilled to have Jackson by their side, but in Jasmine's eyes he served as a temporary consolation rather than a true alternative to Stacey.

Jasmine said her goodbyes to Missy, then headed out the door to meet up with Jackson, who had been waiting patiently in the hallway. "So, you wanna grab some dinner?" he asked.

"I dunno," Jasmine replied. "What did you have in mind?"

"Well, I was kinda in the mood for a home-cooked meal. Do you know anywhere I can get one?"

"There's a really nice, down home restaurant on Shattuck we haven't been to. They serve really good soul food and—"

"Actually," Jackson interrupted, "I was hoping that home-cooked meal would come from your kitchen."

Jackson's words made Jasmine stop dead in her tracks. "I don't cook," she said with a stern expression on her face.

"Um, okay," Jackson replied, waving his hands in the air as though he were surrendering to an army attack.

The last thing Jasmine wanted was to allow Jackson to domesticate her. She already felt uneasy about their relationship, so to think she had allowed him to tie her down was alarming. Yet, she knew she had been sort of harsh with her response so she tried to lighten the mood a bit. "Look, I'm sorry, but I don't cook, okay? I just wanted to make that clear."

"So, you eat takeout everyday?"

"Pretty much. When I'm not on campus I'm at Pleasant Beginnings, so I'm rarely near my kitchen anyway."

"I guess that makes sense."

"Why, do you cook?"

"Yeah. I mean, I'm no Emeril, but I know enough not to starve."

Jackson and Jasmine continued walking down the hall toward the exit, and just when she thought he had dropped the whole cooking thing, he added, "Do you at least bake?"

Jasmine sensed a slight hint of irritation in his voice and found herself annoyed, yet again, by his persistence. "No, I don't bake either. Does that bother you?"

"Yes, it does bother me."

"Why, because I'm not Suzy Homemaker? You were right when you told Missy you couldn't tame me! This is who I am and if you don't like it—"

"Whoa, where is all this hostility coming from?" Jackson stopped walking and looked at Jasmine. They stared at each other for a moment, both visibly agitated, until Jackson broke the tension by saying, "It bothers me that you don't bake because I love cupcakes, that's all."

Jasmine wasn't sure how to respond, but suddenly felt silly for allowing herself to become so upset over nothing. Unable to hold onto her anger any longer, a smile crept out from behind tight lips, and soon Jackson and Jasmine were both looking at each other and laughing.

"You're cute when you're angry, you know that?"

"Whatever," she said, brushing the hair out of her face.

"You know, it was cool seeing you act like that back there."

"Act like what?"

"Loving and nurturing. I never figured you the type, but I can tell that Missy really enjoys having you around."

"Oh, that's nothing."

"No, that's something," insisted Jackson, who looked at Jasmine with a newfound sense of respect and admiration. "Was it your mother who gave you these nurturing qualities?"

"How 'bout we grab some of that soul food I was telling you about," Jasmine quickly replied, as she attempted to change the subject.

Jackson and Jasmine shared a nice meal, then decided to catch the new Chris Tucker flick that had just come out. They were both big fans of the comedian and were excited to see his latest offering. Instead of staying in Berkeley, they decided to venture out to San Francisco for a change, and therefore watched the movie at the Metreon. Chris Tucker didn't disappoint, for the movie proved to be funnier than they had anticipated, leaving them both reeling with laughter as they exited the theater. Jasmine laughed so hard that she had to grab hold of her side to keep it from aching. Jackson placed his arm around her waist, and she leaned into him, giggling softly against his chest. When she raised her head, she saw Stacey and Angel standing a few feet in front of them in the lobby.

Jasmine felt her heart leap into her throat as she watched Angel attempt to help Stacey, who was on crutches, prepare to descend to the lower level of the theater via the escalator. "What's wrong?" asked Jackson.

"Nothing."

"You sure? You look like you just saw a ghost."

"I'm fine," Jasmine replied, dropping her head towards the ground. She tried her best to avoid being spotted by Stacey and Angel, but Angel noticed her before she could run for cover.

"Hey, I thought that was you. How are you doing?"

"Oh, hi Angel," Jasmine replied, her eyes focused on Stacey.

"So, who's your friend?" asked Angel, referring to Jackson.

Before Jasmine could respond, Stacey interjected. "What's up man," he said, nodding toward Jackson.

"How's it going, Stacey," Jackson replied. Jasmine was aware that Jackson knew who Stacey was, but their sudden familiarity made her extremely uncomfortable.

"Angel, this is Jackson. Jackson, this is my girl, Angel."

"Nice to meet you," said Jackson, shaking Angel's hand.

"What did y'all think about the movie?" Stacey asked, directing the question toward Jackson. It was clear to Jasmine that he was attempting to avoid eye contact with her.

"It was cool, better than I expected actually," Jackson replied.

Jasmine already felt uneasy about Stacey seeing her out with Jackson, so when he decided to place his arm around her shoulder, as if to publicly stake his claim, Jasmine became even more perturbed. Shrugging her shoulders, she stepped away from Jackson, forcing his arm to fall back to his side. She did it quickly in hopes that he wouldn't notice what she was trying to do, but he did. "So, what brings you two all the way out to the city?" she asked Stacey, trying to take the focus off of herself and Jackson for a moment

"We could ask you the same thing," he replied. Angel, who was hugged up on him, steadied her face on Jasmine's and smiled as though she were oblivious to the tension in the room.

"Just wanted to get out of Berkeley for a change, I guess," Jasmine replied. She was so uncomfortable that her knees began to buckle.

"Well, we're gonna head home. Y'all have a good night, okay," said Stacey, as he and Angel prepared to leave.

"Bye Jasmine," said Angel, waving. "It was nice meeting you, Jackson," she added before assisting Stacey onto the escalator and down to the lower level of the Metreon. Jasmine stalled for a moment, allowing Stacey and Angel to create some distance between them before she and Jackson followed.

The car ride home was fraught with silence, and Jasmine had no idea what Jackson was thinking. More importantly, she wondered what

Stacey was thinking, seeing her out with Jackson like that. He probably thought they were a couple.

"Here we are," said Jackson, finally pulling up to Jasmine's apartment. She was so consumed with her thoughts that she didn't notice they had made it back to her place. "You want me to carry you to the door?" asked Jackson, who could tell that Jasmine was completely unaware of her surroundings.

"Huh?" she asked, snapping back into reality.

"You seem out of it. You need me to carry you in or something?"

"No…it's just—" Jasmine paused for a moment, searching for the right words to say, then finally asked, "What are we doing, Jackson?"

"We're sitting in my car."

"No, seriously. What is this?"

"I don't understand what you're getting at."

"Us—this re—this relationship, or whatever you want to call it."

Jackson straightened up in his seat and reached for the ignition. He shut off the engine and kept his eyes focused on Jasmine. Neither of them said anything for a while—a long while, until suddenly Jasmine blurted out, "I don't think we should—"

"I want you to be my girlfriend."

"What?"

"I said, I want you to be my girlfriend."

Stunned, Jasmine looked at Jackson, who for once wasn't exhibiting a single ounce of arrogance. Instead, he stared at her with a softness she hadn't seen before, his eyes projecting the same level of intensity she had once found alarming. She started to say something, but was immediately cut off. "I don't—"

"Look, you try to act hard and all, but deep down, you're weak."

"What?"

"You heard me."

"Um, wow. Do you always insult your dates like this? Maybe that worked for you in the past, but it's doing nothing to sway my vote."

"I'm just being real. You asked what it is we're doing, and I'm telling you: we're having a relationship. I know that's hard for you to hear."

"Excuse me? You don't know what you're talking about."

"Oh, I don't, do I? Do you remember what you told me on our first date?"

"I said a lot of things on our first date," snapped Jasmine, who was becoming annoyed.

"Well, let me refresh your memory. We were talking about rumors, and you admitted to dating a lot and basically jumping around from one guy to the next—"

"I am not a hoe! I don't sleep around! I told you that."

"I know you don't, but the point is that you're non-committal. The truth is, you don't even know what a real relationship is, and I think you're too scared to find out."

"You don't know what you're talking about," Jasmine replied, folding her arms across her chest. She stared at the door of her apartment through the car window, and Jackson could sense that she was tuning him out, as she often did whenever she felt the conversation was getting too heavy.

"You're guarded, and you've been guarded for a while," said Jackson, still staring at Jasmine. "Do you realize we've been dating for almost four months now and I barely know anything about your family? I've shared a lot of my background with you, but whenever I try to ask you questions, you shut me down or change the subject."

"I've gotta go," said Jasmine, frantically gathering her purse and coat.

"Wait—" Jackson reached out for her, but she was gone. She slammed the car door before running to her apartment, and all he could do was sit quietly, and watch her walk away.

Chapter 19

The following night, Jasmine lay in bed for hours, pondering everything that had transpired between she and Jackson since the night of their first date. She couldn't believe that the same man who had once repelled her had suddenly become the focal point of her thoughts. It upset her that his presence was beginning to overpower her desire for Stacey, who she had felt drifting further and further away. She wondered if Missy was right about Jackson being the one. Missy had even suggested that Jackson was in love with her, the thought of which excited and scared her, all at the same time. Yet, what scared her even more was the thought that she may actually love him too.

Jasmine hadn't heard a peep out of Jackson since their date, which was a first considering that he had been calling her on a daily basis. Yet, she knew by the way she had stormed out of his car that he was waiting for her to make the next move. She however needed time to think things over, for she still had no clue in which direction she wanted to head.

Jasmine continued to lay in bed, as she allowed her thoughts to drift from Jackson, to Stacey, then Jackson again. She couldn't help but think about what Jackson had said the night of their first date about how she reminded him of a cupcake because of the way she made him feel. She did find his explanation a little cheesy, but it did make sense considering that was the same way she felt when she first saw Stacey. Her mind seemed to travel in circles as it sifted through thoughts of the two men who occupied her world, until it suddenly became interrupted by the sound of an unfamiliar ring tone on her cell phone.

"Hello?" asked Jasmine, curious as to who was calling her so late at night.

"Hello, Jazz?"

"Yeah," she replied, popping straight up in bed. It was a man's voice on the other end of the line, and although it wasn't Jackson's, it definitely sounded familiar. "Who is this?"

"It's Stacey."

Jasmine almost dropped the phone. *Stacey is calling me? I must be dreaming!* "How—how'd you get my number?"

"I got it from Sarah, you know, the staff coordinator at Pleasant Beginnings. She couldn't find your number and called to see if I had it, but ended up finding it while I was on the phone with her. I asked her to give it to me so I could talk to you directly…I hope you don't mind."

"No, not at all," said Jasmine, still confused. Stacey hadn't volunteered in months and was suddenly calling her about a matter related to the facility? "So, what's up?"

"I'm really sorry, Jazz," Stacey began, his voice suddenly growing soft. "I almost can't believe it myself…Missy's dead."

"What!" Jasmine shouted so loudly that Foxy, who had been sitting calmly at the foot of her bed, leaped off frantically when she heard the horror in her voice.

"I'm really sorry, but she passed about an hour ago. Sarah said she suffered another stroke around 10:00 PM—Jazz, you still there?"

"Yeah—yes, I'm still here."

"Like I said, sorry I had to break this to you and so late at night."

"No…thanks, I appreciate it," said Jasmine, feeling woozy.

"I know this is hard for you, but this is hard for me too. I mean, this is really making me think about life, you know." Jasmine was having a difficult time listening to Stacey because she was in shock over the devastating news. She couldn't digest the fact that Missy was dead, or the fact that Stacey, the man of her dreams, was the one delivering the news. It didn't seem real—it couldn't be real, but it was.

"I guess I just feel guilty about dropping out as a volunteer," Stacey continued. "I mean, at the time I felt justified because I needed to devote more time to school, football…and, well, other things happened too…" Stacey's voice trailed off, and Jasmine knew exactly what he meant by "other things." That statement would have provided her the perfect segue to begin discussing their relationship, but his timing couldn't have been worse. "But," he continued, "I now see how valuable that time is we spend helping others."

"Yeah, I know," said Jasmine, who managed to get a few words out, yet even they seemed to roll off her tongue without her knowledge. She tried to push back tears that were beginning to well up in the corners of her eyes, but it was truly becoming a struggle.

"Anyway, I don't want to take up too much of your time," said Stacey, who could sense Jasmine's pain. "I just wanted to let you know that they're holding a memorial service for her at the center this Tuesday night at eight o'clock."

"So soon?" she asked, shocked. "What about her funeral?"

"She asked to be cremated, so her ashes will be interred at the gravesite there."

A tear broke free from Jasmine's hold and rolled down her cheek. The words "gravesite" and "cremation," suddenly made Missy's death seem all too real. Jasmine's body grew weak and she became lightheaded. Foxy, sensing that something was wrong, curled into a ball and rested her warm body on top of Jasmine's feet.

"Hello? You still there?"

"Yeah, I'm here," said Jasmine, wiping the tear from her cheek. "Thanks for filling me in."

"Sure," said Stacey. "By the way, Sarah wants you to call her when you get a chance. She wants to talk to you about Missy and whether or not you want to stay on as a volunteer, but don't worry about all that now. Just take your time. She understands."

"Thanks Stacey."

"Well, you take care, and I'll talk to you later, okay?"

"Okay. Goodnight." Jasmine hung up the phone and sat on her bed, stunned. *Missy's dead?* She had just visited her the other day! If she hadn't introduced Jackson to her then, he would have never gotten an opportunity to meet her.

Jasmine knew the day would come when she would receive a phone call like that, but she never thought it would come so soon—or from Stacey. She had longed for the day when he would call her on the phone, but never in her wildest dreams had thought it would be under such negative circumstances. As for Missy, Jasmine had thought for sure she'd at least be around to see her graduate. Missy often talked about how she would attend her graduation and help her celebrate, even if she had to do so in a wheelchair…yet, it was clear that God had other plans for her.

Chapter 20

The day following Missy's death was a Monday, and Jasmine seemed to pass through it in a haze. She only had two classes to attend, which was good because she could barely think straight. Although Missy had been bed ridden since her previous stroke, her spirit and energy never faltered. Thus, her death had been so sudden and unexpected, much like Jasmine's mother's, that it made it very difficult for her to accept. Still in shock about the whole situation, Jasmine tried her best to get through the day by masking her pain, with denial making it easier to do so.

As soon as Jasmine heard the Campanile clock signal that it was two o'clock, she grabbed her backpack and headed out the door of her last class. To her surprise, she found Jackson standing outside the door of her lecture hall. "Hey. Good to see you," she said, somewhat startled by his presence. "I've been meaning to call you."

"Really? When?" Jackson leaned against the wall with his hands placed firmly inside the pockets of his loose-fitting jeans. He was dressed casually, which was unusual for him. Remembering that Mondays were his days off, Jasmine realized that he was dressed down because he wasn't coming from class, and was therefore only there to see her. Yet, by the look on his face, he didn't seem too thrilled.

"Um, later," she replied, still trying to read his expression. Jasmine couldn't tell if Jackson was just tired or pissed off that she hadn't called him since their last date, which had ended on a sour note. She therefore decided to tell him about Missy's passing so that he could see that she had other things on her mind aside from their conversation a few nights ago. "I have something to tell you."

"What's up?"

"Missy passed away late last night. I got a call from—I was informed of it yesterday."

"Why didn't you call me?"

"It was late."

"It's never too late with me, you know that."

Jasmine remained silent and slowly dropped her head towards the floor. She really wasn't in the mood to deal with Jackson. Their relationship was just too much for her to think about, especially with Missy gone. She couldn't stop thinking about how much she was going to miss her. She also couldn't stop thinking about Stacey, and how much she wanted to talk to him. Since he had volunteered at the assisted living facility and knew Missy well, she figured he would be able to relate to her better than anyone.

"I think I'm gonna head home now. I'm tired and really just want to be alone," said Jasmine, finally lifting her head to look at Jackson.

"Alone? Now?" Jackson stared back at her, frowning. There was no question that he was pissed off at this point.

"Yes, now!" she replied, angry. "You're not the only thing going on in my life right now you know. Why does everything have to be so personal with you? This doesn't even concern you!"

"Yes, this does concern me! You concern me! Why do you think we're in this relationship?"

"I don't know," Jasmine replied, throwing her arms in the air. She was tired, distraught, and wanted to go home, so she turned and slowly began to walk away.

Once Jasmine made it outside of Wheeler auditorium, she had to hold her hand in front of her face to shield her eyes from the sun, which was beating down intensely. She squinted to keep from going blind as she trekked across campus toward Bancroft Avenue where the buses and campus shuttles departed. Deciding to forgo a cab ride for once, Jasmine hopped inside the bus as soon as it arrived. Before she could find a seat, the front of her jeans began to jiggle, as her cell phone vibrated inside her pocket.

"Hello?"

"It's me, Jackson."

Jasmine rolled her eyes and let out a huge sigh. "Yes?"

"I'm sorry, okay? I know you're going through a tough time now and I should be more sensitive."

There was a long pause, for Jasmine wasn't sure how to respond. She felt overwhelmed by her emotions and wanted to rid herself of Jackson, for he seemed to add just one more complicated dimension to her already troubled life. "That's cool," she finally replied, wondering if she were doing the right thing.

"Look, I know you said you wanted to be alone, but I just want to be there for you. Let me at least take you to dinner."

Jasmine felt a strange game of tug of war start to take place inside her mind. One side told her to leave Jackson alone before she wound up hurt, for she still wasn't sure if he could be trusted. Besides, she had been forced to deal with tragedy on her own since she was a little girl, so she saw no reason why she couldn't just be left alone to mourn her good friend's passing. Yet, another side told her to open up and let Jackson in, but doing that would mean relinquishing all hope for herself and Stacey. Although she appeared tough on the outside, inside she felt sad, scared, and alone.

"Okay," Jasmine said after another long pause.

"Okay what?"

"Okay, I'll go to dinner with you."

"Great," Jackson replied, his voice laced with hope. "I'll swing by later to pick you up."

"All right."

****

Later that evening, Jackson took Jasmine to dinner as promised. They were eating dinner outside on the rooftop of Café Durant, when Jasmine decided to pull a fresh pack of cigarettes out of her purse. She set her lighter on the table and began to peel back the plastic on the package when she suddenly felt the warmth of Jackson's palm on her hand.

"I know you're not about to light up."

"Why not?"

"Because for one, we're in a restaurant, and two, I thought you quit."

"Who said I quit? Did I tell you I quit? Just because you confiscated most of my stash—and yes, I know you took the carton off my dresser in my apartment when I wasn't looking—that doesn't mean that I've quit."

Jasmine managed to pry the pack open and pull out a cigarette before Jackson could respond. The waiter however spotted her from across the room and stalled her efforts just as she began to raise the cigarette to her lips.

"Excuse me, miss, there's no smoking here."

"But we're outside," said Jasmine, whipping her head around to address the waiter who had decided to involve himself in her business.

"Technically, yes, but this is still a restaurant, and California law states—"

"I know all about California law," she quipped, forcefully shoving the cigarette and lighter back inside her purse. "You ready?" she asked, turning toward Jackson.

"Yeah, we can go."

"Let's," she said before angrily grabbing her things as she and Jackson prepared to leave. Jackson threw a wad of ones on top of the table for the tip and the two of them headed down the stairs and out onto the street.

"Do you want to talk about it?" he asked, placing one arm around her shoulder.

"No," she replied, before throwing his arm off. "I think I just need to be alone for a while. Missy's service is tomorrow and—"

"I'll go with you."

"No!" Jasmine yelled so loudly that she startled the man who stood a few feet away from them at the corner of the block, causing him to drop the aluminum cans he had meticulously picked out of the trash can. "Look," she said, modifying the tone of her voice, which had been unnecessarily harsh. "It's nothing personal, really."

Jackson stared at her incredulously and rubbed his goatee. The tension between them combined with the stress and depression that was raging inside her only served to increase her yearning to spark up. She retrieved her lighter and pack of cigarettes again, but this time Jackson couldn't take it, and knocked both items out of her hand.

"You're not smoking anymore, you hear me?" he said, enraged. A part of Jasmine felt frightened by Jackson's sudden burst of emotion, while another part of her was turned on. "I understand you're going through a rough time, but I'm tired of you looking for a way out instead of just confronting your issues head on," he said as he began fiddling inside his pocket for the keys to his car. Jackson pressed a button on the remote key panel and the faint flash of two headlights could be seen in the near distance. "Come on," he said, before hurriedly taking off down the street.

Jackson was angry, the proof evident in his steps, which had become fast and determined. Jasmine followed, her feet shuffling rapidly in an effort to keep up. Once they finally made it to where his car was parked, Jackson opened the passenger side door before walking around the back to enter through the driver's side. She fought to wipe the smirk off her face before he entered the car. For once she had succeeded at annoying him as much as he had her.

Once they made it back to Jasmine's place, Jackson followed her inside, claiming he had to use the bathroom. Yet, they were making out before she could lock the door behind them. Passionately hugging and kissing, the two of them headed toward Jasmine's bedroom, which was located near the back of her apartment. They were so caught up in the moment that they ended up falling onto the bed, not realizing that Foxy was lying there taking a nap.

"Meowww!" Jasmine felt Foxy's claws dig into her lower back, forcing her to sit up immediately, which also caused Jackson to rise.

"Ouch!" Jasmine shrieked, while rubbing the spot where Foxy had scratched her.

"She got you good," said Jackson, examining her wound. "You're bleeding."

Jasmine traced the cut on her back then looked at her fingers, which were covered in blood. "I have some band aids in the bathroom. Can you look inside the medicine cabinet?"

Jackson stood up and headed toward the bathroom to get the band aids, then returned a few moments later to nurse Jasmine's wounds. "All better," he said after applying the bandage. "That was a real mood killer."

"Tell me about it," she replied, smoothing her tousled hair with her hands.

"But, we can finish where we left off," added Jackson in typical male fashion. He leaned forward and cupped her face with his hands, but she pushed on his chest to stop him from laying one on her.

"I think we should stop," said Jasmine, knowing that was the last thing Jackson or any man wanted to hear. Yet, things were getting too heavy for her, especially since she still had unresolved feelings for Stacey, and was trying to cope with Missy's death.

Letting out a woeful sigh, Jackson retreated to one corner of the bed and sat down. "Okay, if you say so," he said.

Watching his head fall into his hands, Jasmine could tell that he wasn't really "okay" with it. "This is a really hard time for me right now—"

"I know, I know," said Jackson, cutting Jasmine off. "Really, it's cool. You don't have to explain." He glanced at his watch while she searched the room for Foxy, who was hiding underneath the vanity for fear that she would be crushed again. "I guess I should get going," he said, twisting the watch around his wrist.

"Actually, you can stay a while…if you want," said Jasmine, hesitantly. She hated feeling vulnerable, yet feared she'd melt into a puddle of tears if Jackson were to leave her alone.

"I would, but I have an early class in the morning."

"You can spend the night," Jasmine blurted out, not realizing how enticing her offer sounded. She saw Jackson's face light up like a Christmas tree and knew then that she needed to qualify her statement to clear up the misunderstanding. "I mean, sleep over. You can just sleep here."

Jackson's eyebrows, which had risen up to his hairline, slowly fell back into place once he realized that Jasmine wasn't asking to have the slumber party he intended. "Oh, okay," he said, finally getting the message.

Jackson and Jasmine spent the rest of the evening watching television and laughing about random stuff, until finally, they prepared for bed. Jasmine washed her face and pulled her hair back into a ponytail before slipping into a cute pants set from Victoria's Secret. Jackson took off his shirt and jeans, leaving just his boxers and a white tank top on. As Jasmine emerged from the bathroom, Jackson stared into her mascara-free eyes as though he were just seeing her for the first time.

With a five o'clock shadow creeping up on his face, Jackson looked just as unmade up as Jasmine. Both of them, though not at their best, seemed to be looking at each other's true self. Jasmine stood in front of him, silent, her face bare. Jackson took a deep breath and began speaking in a more serious, somber tone than Jasmine was used to hearing. "You look beautiful," he said.

Confused and self-conscious, Jasmine ran one hand through her disheveled ponytail and then across the side of her bare face. "Thanks," she replied, not sure if she should believe him, although he sounded sincere. The seriousness of Jackson's tone and the intense look in his eyes made her feel uneasy, scared even. She continued to stand in front of him, frozen, until Foxy began to climb up her leg. "Down girl," she said, brushing Foxy off, who purred loudly before slowly retreating back underneath the vanity. Jackson climbed into Jasmine's bed, and she did the same. The two of them lay stiff on their backs as they stared up at the ceiling, quiet. Neither of them said anything for a while, and Jasmine began to wonder if having him stay over was a good idea. After all, he was supposed to be helping her relax, not tense up.

"You know," Jackson began, "I imagined us in bed together the moment we met. I just never thought it would be like this."

"Shut up," said Jasmine, playfully hitting his arm.

"All jokes aside, this is cool though. It's definitely a first for me, but it's cool."

"Well, I'm glad to know you're 'cool,' with everything."

"I just want you to know that I'm really glad you're in my life," Jackson said suddenly, his tone shifting almost instantly. Jasmine heard the change in his voice and it made her legs stiffen. "I wasn't expecting anything more than a degree when I came to Cal," he continued, "But you've made this experience even more worthwhile." Pausing for a moment, Jackson looked over at Jasmine and into her eyes as her head lay on the pillow next to his. "I've never felt this strongly about any woman before…although, now that I think about it, I've never really allowed myself to get to know a woman like this before. In the past it was just—"

"Hit it and quit it," said Jasmine, finishing his sentence.

"Um, that's one way of putting it."

As much as Jasmine tried to deny it, she really had grown close to Jackson. Here he was opening up to her, while she leaned on him for support. The arrogant and cocky person that was presented to her a year prior had disappeared, leaving behind the strong, caring man that lay next to her. It all seemed so strange, and Jasmine still wasn't sure what to make of it all. As she lay next to him, full of uncertainty, he surprised her by drawing her in close, enabling her to rest her head on his chest. She could hear the soft thump of his beating heart, and the sweet sound caused her to feel conflicted even more, for a part of her wanted to kick him out and face her pain alone, while another part wanted to remain wrapped up in his arms, warm and sheltered from the pain that sought to pull her down.

As much as Jasmine wanted to believe in Jackson, their whole relationship was becoming all too reminiscent of her time with Demetri. He too had once appeared genuine, which is why she decided to give him a chance. Yet, he used the death of her mother to break down her walls, only to later deceive her, and she feared that Jackson was using Missy's death in the same way.

"I really want to go to the service with you tomorrow."

"Um…about that," Jasmine began, making sure to choose her words carefully. She knew how persistent Jackson could be, so if he sensed that she was pushing him away, he would insist on going. Thus, she knew she had to make up an excuse and present it to him in the nicest way possible to keep him from feeling rejected. "I think I'd rather just go alone," she continued.

"Jasmine—"

"Look, it's nothing personal, really. Missy was like a second mother to me, so this is very hard. I really just want to attend the service alone so I can process it all." There was dead silence for a moment, and Jasmine wasn't sure if Jackson was taking it all in, or getting angry. She therefore decided to further explain herself so that he could better understand where she was coming from. "This service tomorrow is really sacred. It means more to me than you know."

Jackson let out a deep sigh, then said, "I don't understand, but I guess I can accept it."

"Thanks," she replied, trying to sound sweet. "I really appreciate that. I promise I'll make it up to you."

"How?" asked Jackson, almost immediately.

"I'll call you as soon as it's over. We can meet at Café Milano and grab some hot cocoa, maybe a little dessert…"

"Mmm, that sounds good," said Jackson, sounding more satisfied with the situation.

Jasmine felt relieved knowing that she didn't have to figure everything out just then, for as much as she wanted to trust Jackson, a small part of her still longed for Stacey. Instead of worrying about how everything was going to work out, she resolved to go to sleep, nestled comfortably in Jackson's arms.

Chapter 21

Jasmine prepared for Missy's memorial service and fought back bouts of sorrow as she selected an outfit to wear. She had told Jackson she didn't want him to come and was trying to remain cool, calm, and collected, but slowly she was beginning to unravel. Wiping the tears from her eyes, she slipped into a black baby doll dress, then slid her feet inside a pair of hot pink stilettos. Missy was a character, and Jasmine knew that the last thing she would have wanted was for her to go around sulking, draped in black. Thus, she chose to don her loudest pair of shoes as a symbol of Missy's undying spirit, and topped it off with a matching pink charm bracelet and a hot pink hand bag.

At seven thirty-five, Jasmine heard the cab she reserved for the evening pull up outside her apartment. She kissed Foxy goodbye, then headed out the door. The ride to the service was a silent one, for Jasmine felt like she would explode into a million little pieces if she dared utter a single word. Her anxiety intensified as the driver finally pulled into the parking lot of Pleasant Beginnings. The reality of Missy's death was becoming unbearable, and Jasmine did her best to maintain her composure.

Candles lined the walkway that led toward the facility, which Jasmine figured was something special they had setup for the service. As she slowly made her way towards the entrance of the building, she thought back to the many times she had taken that same walk up the driveway to spend time with Missy. It was funny how differently she felt this time around, for it seemed that even her feet, which begrudgingly made their way up the path, also knew that this walk was leading her to something different.

As Jasmine entered the building, she felt a flood of emotions pour over her. First it was the loss of Missy that engulfed her, then thoughts of her mother, which came rushing back to her in a flood. She also thought about Jackson and how she was so unsure of her feelings for him…and of course, she thought about Stacey, for the facility was where she had spent most of her time getting to know him. As she struggled with various emotions, her mind got lost in a fog, and she had to take a moment to orient herself. Once she returned to the moment, she realized Stacey and Angel were standing in front of her in the lobby.

"Hello Jasmine," Angel spoke softly.

"Hey," Jasmine replied, suddenly feeling queasy.

"Hey Jazz, good to see you," said Stacey, looking at her with watery eyes. "I wish we could meet under different circumstances though."

Before Jasmine could respond, Angel chimed in, "We're really sorry about your loss," then looked at Jasmine with a glum expression on her face. For a second it appeared as though she were going to cry, but she fought back the tears and stated in a lower tone, "This reminds me of when my grandmother passed away six months ago." Stacey reached for her hand, and Jasmine, feeling more alone than ever, suddenly grew numb.

Everything Jasmine ever felt for Stacey vanished in that instance, for it became clearer than before, that the two of them would never be. Seeing him reach for Angel in that tender moment awakened her to the reality of the situation, for no longer could she entertain thoughts of having a relationship with a guy who couldn't be there for her in a time of need. Missy had been right all along, and it seemed fitting that the facility—the same place in which Jasmine had been scolded about her infatuation with Stacey, and the same place she had developed feelings for him, would also be the place she would finally relinquish her pursuit of him.

The chapel was packed with many of the home's residents, as well as a few faces Jasmine had never seen before. As Stacey and Angel took seats near the back of the room, Jasmine began to follow suit, but was stopped by the minister, who stood near the front of the room and beckoned for her to approach. She looked over at Stacey and Angel, bewildered, but they simply urged her to follow the minister's lead. She could feel every eye in the room on her as she took slow strides down the aisle.

"Good evening young lady. It's Jasmine, right?" asked the minister.

"Yes."

"We would like for you to sit up front. Please, have a seat." The minister pointed toward a seat in the front row, miles away from where Stacey and Angel sat. Jasmine reluctantly took it, still unsure as to why she was being singled out. The minister didn't offer any explanation, and took to the podium to commence the service.

The minister took a few moments to ask God to look after Missy's loved ones, as they began their journey toward overcoming the pain of loss, then finished his prayer with a resounding "Amen," from the crowd. He proceeded with the service, and Jasmine felt herself zone in and out as she tried to fight back tears that were starting to well up inside her. Spending time with Missy had enriched her life in many ways, so the idea of no longer having her as a fixture hurt her to the core. She shifted uncomfortably in the pew, and watched as the minister displayed a piece of paper to the audience. "Ladies and gentlemen," he began, "The following note was found in Missy Mae Holden's room after she passed away. It's a poem she wrote, and I feel the message

embedded in it is not only fitting for the moment, but something I
believe she would have liked for us to share with you." The minister
adjusted his glasses and proceeded to read. "The poem is entitled, 'My
Life,' and goes as follows:

> *Molded by the hands of my creator,*
> *Life begins in the womb,*
> *And ends decades later.*
> *Like the ticking of a clock,*
> *Time passes by;*
> *People come and go,*
> *But love never dies.*
> *When the rivers dry up,*
> *And life withers away,*
> *It'll be the time we spent together*
> *That will always stay."*

A salty tear rolled down Jasmine's cheek and touched the corner
of her mouth before curving downward, wrapping its way underneath
her chin. She felt sharp pains shoot through her left breast, as though
Missy's hand were grabbing hold of her heart and squeezing it, while the
minister read the words of her poem. Missy, who had always spoken
about the importance of love and companionship, had truly lended her
voice to the poem, as the message resonated loud and clear with
Jasmine. Her words proved compelling to others as well, for sobs could
be heard coming from all corners of the chapel.

Deep down, Jasmine knew that what Missy said was true, for
love was the most important thing in life, although somewhere down the
line she had allowed fear to cripple her ability to accept and exhibit it
toward others. All Jackson wanted was to be her man and support her
through the good and bad times, but instead of appreciating him, she
tossed him aside for a foolish dream that she now knew would never
come true. Yet, it hadn't simply been her affection for Stacey that caused
her to diss Jackson, for it was ultimately her fear of love and

commitment that impeded her ability to let down her guard. Demetri had hurt her more than she ever thought possible, but sitting alone at Missy's funeral when she could have had Jackson by her side, made her realize how she was still allowing him to get the best of her.

The minister switched gears for a moment and focused his eyes directly on Jasmine's. "Everyone, I would like to take this opportunity to introduce you to a special young lady we have sitting in our presence this evening. Jasmine Fairchild was Missy's volunteer caretaker, and the two of them shared a very special bond." Jasmine could hear people shuffling as they turned to face her. She slumped down in the pew, steadying her attention on the minister as he continued. "Miss Holden lived a humble life and cared deeply for others. She had a beautiful spirit, and brought great joy to the lives of those she encountered."

The audience expressed their agreement with the minister's favorable depiction of Missy by responding with a concerted "Mhmm," and Jasmine nodded her head in agreement.

"Missy was the last of three children," explained the minister, "And she leaves behind no siblings, no spouse, or any children of her own. However, as I mentioned before, she shared a close bond with one of our very own volunteers, whom she referred to as her daughter."

A tight lump formed in the back of Jasmine's throat, and she lost the battle of the tears, which rushed down her face like waves of water that had broken free from a weakened dam. "It is Miss Holden's wish," concluded the minister, "as expressed to the staff members of the facility, that everything she owns of value be passed on to Miss Fairchild." Gasping, Jasmine couldn't believe what the minister said. She was in such disbelief that she barely heard his closing words. "The relationship that Miss Fairchild succeeded in establishing with Miss Holden is one that we encourage all our volunteers to form," expressed the minister. "The fact that their bond surpassed generational barriers is truly amazing. Miss Fairchild has truly shown us how to love one another."

Knowing that she'd never get the chance to speak to Missy again, Jasmine's silent tears erupted into violent sobs, making it impossible for her to remain still. Stacey and Angel rushed to console her, and she poured out her pain onto them. Little did they know, Jasmine was not only shedding tears for Missy, but for herself as well. She couldn't believe how foolish she had been, and knew it was time she truly devote herself to Jackson, or risk losing him for good.

A few people took to the podium once the minister opened the floor to the audience, but Jasmine didn't hear a word they said, for she was still caught up in her own emotions. Minutes later, the minister closed the entire ceremony with a prayer, and the audience began to disperse. Jasmine remained seated in the front pew, unable to move, until Angel assisted her in getting up.

"It's okay," said Angel, patting her on the head.

"Yeah, it'll be all right," added Stacey, who stood on the other side of her.

Angel helped Jasmine to her feet before escorting her out of the chapel, and Stacey followed them on crutches. Her feet felt like lead, as she slowly dragged them up the aisle, down the hallway, and outside to where Stacey's car was parked. He and Angel offered her a ride home, which she gratefully accepted.

The ride home was a blur for Jasmine, who found it extremely difficult to breathe through a stuffed up nose. She didn't even realize they had made it to her place until Angel shut off the engine. Stacey, who sat in the passenger seat, turned his head around to offer some final words of encouragement. "Our thoughts and prayers are with you," he said.

"Thanks," Jasmine replied before stepping outside the car.

Chapter 22

As Jasmine entered Café Milano, she thought of the irony surrounding her situation. Just as she had let go of her feelings for Stacey at the facility where she had fallen for him, she was also choosing to express her feelings for Jackson in the same place she had initially rejected him. It added beautiful symmetry to her life, so she thought, for it enabled her to gain a fresh start, no longer allowing her past to get the best of her.

"Hey there," she said to Jackson, after spying him seated at a table, sipping on a cup of hot chocolate.

"Hey, how was it?" he asked before rising out of his chair. Jasmine threw her arms around his neck and squeezed him tightly. "What was that for?"

"Nothing," she said, although she realized that after all they'd been through, there was no way he would ever take her new affectionate attitude towards him as "nothing." "Well, actually, it was for something," she added with a hint of nervousness in her voice. Jackson stared at her with a puzzled look on his face as she continued, "I've been thinking of how sweet you've been through all this, and I can't really say that I've been the same."

"That's okay. I know this is a tough time—"

"That's no excuse for my behavior."

Jackson had no idea Jasmine wasn't just referring to her recent behavior, but her attitude towards him overall. Yet, the fact that she was offering some ounce of remorse was enough to make the tension in his face subside. "Well, I appreciate that," he said, smiling faintly. He continued to stare at her, and she could sense there was more on his mind. After a pregnant pause, he stated, "I know this sounds crazy, 'cause I just saw you the other day, but you seem different."

"Yeah, well, tonight changed a lot of things for me," she said, taking a seat at the table.

Jackson raised his eyebrow, for he still didn't understand how she could change her tune so quickly, but decided to let it go. "You want anything?" he asked.

"No thanks."

"I'm gonna go order a cupcake. I'll be right back."

Jasmine remained seated at the table and watched as Jackson headed toward the cashier to place his order. There was so much on her mind that she wanted to share with him—things she had kept from him for months, but she knew she needed to take it slow because he already seemed confused and would just end up feeling overwhelmed. Sighing, she looked over at him wistfully and thought how funny it was that she had long been unsure of her feelings for him, but was now absolutely certain that she wanted to be with him and only him.

Although a part of Jasmine was hopeful for the future, another part of her was still a little scared, for she had yet to face her propensity to sabotage potentially good relationships. She therefore knew she was going to have to make some serious changes in her life in order for their relationship to work. *Where should I begin?* she asked herself. *I think I'll start by quitting smoking, for good,* she thought, her eyes still focused on Jackson. He leaned against the counter as he waited for his order, and Jasmine continued the silent conversation she was having with herself. *I should also acquire some culinary skills…*She paused in the midst of her reflective moment as Jackson glanced over to look at her. Their eyes locked and he smiled, suddenly putting her at ease. *I just need to find a really good recipe*, she concluded, *And learn how to bake a killer cupcake.*

Johnnie Girl Publishing
www.JGirlPub.com

www.ingramcontent.com/pod-product-compliance
Lightning Source LLC
Chambersburg PA
CBHW020625250626
47154CB00004B/1675